Collateral Damage

48 Stories

Nancy Ludmerer

Cover photo by Chrystie Sherman

Snake~Nation~Press
Valdosta, Georgia

Snake Nation Press is a small non-profit press dedicated to publishing literature in all its myriad forms.

Published by
Snake~Nation~Press
110 West Force Street
Valdosta, Georgia 31601
www.snakenationpress.org

Printed and bound in the United States of America.

ISBN: 978-1-7346810-7-9

Snake~Nation~Press
Thanks
Barbara Passmore & The Price-Campbell Foundation
The Georgia Council for the Arts
Gloria & Wilby Coleman
Lowndes/Valdosta Arts Commission
Dean Poling & *The Valdosta Daily Times*
Blake Ellis
Our Subscribers

Snake Nation Press, the only independent literary press in south Georgia, publishes two issues of *Snake Nation Review,* a book of poetry by a single author each year, and a book of fiction by a single author each year. Unsolicited submissions of fiction, essays, art, and poetry are welcome throughout the year but will not be returned unless a stamped, self-addressed envelope is included. We encourage simultaneous submissions and email entries to snake.nation.press@gmail.com.

Subscriptions
Individuals $30
Institutions $40
Foreign $40
Sample Copy $12 (includes shipping)

Contents

Part I - Collateral Damage

Collateral Damage / 8
After Happiness / 9
Waiting / 11
First Night / 12
After the Wedding / 14
St. Malo / 15
Hal's Sleep Showroom / 18
So Gentle You Don't Feel It /22
Ecosystem / 24
Learning to Dive in Bonaire / 26
Reading, Writing, Arithmetic / 28
Fathers / 30
Hide-and-Seek / 32
Foley Square, July 2019 / 36
Clementine / 38
Family Day / 40
No Offense / 43
Ski In/ Ski Out / 46
Complicity / 47
At the Pool Party for My Niece's Graduation from Middle School /49
End Game / 50
Now You See It / 51
Do You Remember Me? / 54
The Decision / 56
A Bohemian Memoir / 57
13 Tips for Photographing Your Nephew's Bar Mitzvah When You Still Can't Forgive Your Brother-In-Law / 65

Part II - In The Repair Shop

Tiffy / 70

Breakfast with Henry / 71

How My Mother Lost Her Voice and
Gave Me Mine / 74

Eavesdropping / 75

Susceptible to Scratches / 77

Security Device / 79

Adventureland / 80

Bar Mitzvah / 87

Destiny / 88

Spirit of the Staircase / 90

Reasons Why You Should or Shouldn't
Sleep With Your Son's Piano Teacher / 97

Tale of a Fish / 100

Cara Cara / 103

Morris and Cleo / 104

Heirloom / 105

Yard Sale / 106

In Memory of Maisie / 108

Fifty Cents A Cap / 110

Yahrzeit / 111

Mayim / 114

Dream Job / 116

There I Will Take Your Hand / 125

Acknowledgments and Thanks / 128

About the Author / 130

In loving memory of my parents,
Helen and Morris Ludmerer,

and my friend,
Nancy Zafris

I
Collateral Damage

Collateral Damage

For weeks, the fly got the better of them. When they thought it was gone it reappeared, all abuzz. First that fly witnessed disagreement, then yelling, then coldness, turning away, weeping, someone locked in a bathroom, a swollen lip. Hard objects breaking against walls. The fly, to its surprise, was not the target of any of these attacks, not even the last, which for the fly was a first.

"With humans," it mused, "even more than with us, every day is bloodshed."

When the woman left, the fly pondered a moment too long: go or stay?

Then the man pounced.

After Happiness

When your twelve-year-old son asks why you aren't happy, you begin by telling him he's wrong. You shake your head and say you're not unhappy but the minute the double negative escapes your lips you have to agree (although not to him) that you don't sound happy, and, when he adds you haven't looked happy in weeks, you say you are but it's not a you-look-happy happy.

Hours later, after he's gone out, you look in the mirror over your vanity. You try to remember when the last time was that you were truly happy. Not a "this is all we've ever wanted is for you to be happy" happy, and not a guy asking you after sex if you're happy happy, and not the glum expression you'd wear like a mask when your parents visited you at university to remind them about their personal responsibility for the Vietnam War and racism in America, hiding that you were really (really) personally happy.

It wasn't even travel happy, when you walked through the mists to Mont St.Michel before the tide came in happy and celebrated with Cancale oysters, and it wasn't strictly speaking a food happy, not a ripe plums happy, peaches, green grapes you burst with your teeth happy, nor camembert-brie-St. Andre happy, and not a please don't talk to me while I eat this happy, and it's not even holding your newborn happy, singing him songs you thought you had forgotten happy, seeing his midnight eyes consume you happy, nor is it racing to post-natal exercise with him in his carriage and an old lady passing by saying enjoy it, it will never be this good again happy, and it's not the everything will be all right now that I'm on Zoloft happy, and it's not the everything will be all right once the Zoloft is out of my system and I regain the feeling in my clitoris happy.

Instead of these it's a single moment in 1970 after seeing the movie *Women in Love*. You were in a restaurant in the West 50s, thinking about how Glenda

Jackson was considered a great actress without being classically beautiful. Eating chocolate fondue.

Maybe it was the serotonin or Glenda Jackson, but you turned to your companion, the French horn player, your soul mate (although at the time you thought him too predictable and lamented that you could finish his sentences), and said,"I am so happy." But what happened after – whether because of the embarrassed look on his face or something about D.H. Lawrence or something else, still unknown to you – was that being happy suddenly became something lonely and solitary, something even your companion who knew you so well could not understand. Something you were not prepared or able to share with anyone after that, something so private it needed to retreat behind locked doors and reflect against blank walls, and something ephemeral so ephemeral that as soon as you gave voice to it, it vanished.

Waiting

As David unbuttoned her blouse in the studio apartment on West 12th, Maya wondered if they waited too long. They waited in high school, jammed into a broom closet, kisses sucking the ammonia-scented air. They waited on a bench on a traffic island on Queens Boulevard, jeans unzipped, hands skimming hair and flesh. They waited rolled in a blanket in Central Park during rained-out performances of *Henry V*. When a cop said, "Move it, kids" they moved.

At universities in different cities, they waited, too. Could semen on a girl's thigh make her pregnant? Did the air kill it or what? Once in a borrowed apartment in Philadelphia, he unwrapped a condom and filled it with water, checking for leaks. By then they were laughing too hard and went out for a pint of rum-raisin ice cream instead. Afterwards, they slept so soundly, he almost missed his bus to Ithaca.

Now, on West 12th Street, as he moved his lips to her breast, as she felt his tongue begin the slow circling that once had driven her wild, she heard everything: the faucet drip; the shifting of the unwashed dishes from their dinner; the toilet refilling. They were free to take as long as they wished, to be completely naked, to keep the lights on or off, to do it on the shag rug or the corduroy sofa bed.

Later, she would remember that moment when, imperceptibly, she pulled back.

How could she tell him they waited too long?"

First Night

The loft bedroom was filled with snow, and Joyce looked at me with dismay as if it were my fault that both the owner and the sole Tripadvisor reviewer had lied and our quaint ski chalet, perfect (so they said) for a romantic honeymoon, was uninhabitable in January.

Joyce disappeared down the wooden ladder-like staircase, and I heard the motor of our Zipcar and descended the ladder as fast as I could and raced outside, horrified that my wife was about to abandon me on the night of our wedding (small as it was, in the courthouse, still a wedding) but she honked for me to get in and I clambered gratefully into the front seat just as the motor sputtered and died. She tried to start the car again, gripping the wheel tight, her hands bare – where were her gloves? – except for the topaz ring I'd given her, the only jewelry she wore. She had a different topaz ring once, which her father gave her when she turned sixteen. A popular classmate had admired it and asked to try it on, and Joyce never saw it again. The classmate insisted she'd given it back. "Weren't there any witnesses?" I'd asked, when Joyce first told me the story. "No one who believed me," she said.

When the motor failed a third time, I said, "Let me try" and when it failed twice more, I said: "Let's call Triple A." But we had no cell service and no WiFi, and Joyce began to cry and said she hadn't wanted to tell me this way and didn't know how it happened but she was already pregnant and hadn't said anything before lest I think she was trying to trap me and I confessed I'd suspected as much or at least wondered why she was so silent and kept the window half-open from Staten Island to Vermont and then she stopped crying and the only sound was the ghostly whisper of snowflakes.

"We may as well stay," I murmured into her soft hair after a long while, "drink our wine" – at which she shook her head vehemently – "and sleep in the kitchen beside the potbellied stove," and she replied that there were plenty of blankets in the hall cupboard, at least according to the owner's instructions, which she now unfolded and peered at in her lap, using the light from the car's mirrored sun visor above her seat.

When I woke during the night, she wasn't beside me. I lay there wondering whether the coffee and bread and milk we brought would be enough for breakfast, and whether we'd get cell service or get the car to start, and after I heard the toilet flush, but she didn't reappear, I climbed the wooden ladder to the loft bedroom and there was my wife, on the top rung, her lovely hair disheveled, eating snow.

After the Wedding

We're 55 and just married, and I for one get embarrassed when people congratulate us too heartily, as if they see and smell our bodies, not taut but glistening with afterglow, pungent with vanilla-scented lubricant. "Do not deny me," Tony murmured that first time, his hands rough but kind.

We married quickly. Tony, a widower, said I was unlike other divorced women because I wasn't *bitter*. Tonight, from our bench on the boardwalk, we're dazed by the full moon, its half-smile anointing our marriage, our three-day honeymoon. Until three boys stop in front of us – one with pomaded dark hair, a crooner's part; another with hair in a bun (total weirdo!), and the third a shadow in the moon-licked darkness.

Crooner tries to bum a cigarette off Tony.

I say quickly, "We don't smoke," trying to avoid a conflagration, but Tony rises in fury, won't let it go. "Have you been to a hospital, seen what it does?"

"I've been," Crooner says. "I'm twenty. I can do what I want." The guy with the bun sniggers but the third asks softly, "Did you lose someone?"

"Did I lose someone? Did I? My wife. A nurse, who didn't smoke, but died from being around people like you."

"Let's go," the third guy begs. But Crooner turns and points at me. "I thought she was your wife, pops."

Later, I will not deny him.

But his words "my wife" will lie between us, and a smoky haze, like fog, descends.

St. Malo

I'm at the edge of the hotel's parking area, looking north. An endless expanse of grey sand and distant blue-black waves. Andrew has gone to register. It's our last night in Brittany, a three-star hotel, known for its menu as well as its view: my favorite, oysters, and Andrew's, lamb. Andrew is pleased with the room he's reserved for us, with a small balcony overlooking the sea.

I'm eager to get on the beach while it's still light but figure I should wait for Andrew. A door slams in the hotel. Through the hotel's picture window, I see the clerk waving her hands, Andrew pounding fist into palm. I don't want to witness this argument. I don't care what it's about. Is that bad to say? Although never directed at me, Andrew's anger is a thing to behold. It can be exhausting. I find the steps, remove my sandals, and descend, drop them beside the bottom rung. The beach is long and wide, and for a moment, it's all mine. *Almost.* A black-bearded man, 60-ish perhaps, in a T-shirt, with hairy, muscular arms, pushes a woman in a wheelchair, heading west, parallel to the hotel. Her hair shines white-blonde to her shoulders, topped by a beret of indeterminate color – navy or black. Blankets hide the rest. I trek in my bare feet, loving the feel of the sand, dry but coarser than at home in Long Beach. I keep a polite distance, or what I think is a polite distance, but perhaps not distant enough. The man glances in my direction, then leans over his companion. He maneuvers the wheelchair until they're heading directly out to sea. It's a long way out, and there's plenty of sand to cross. I want to get closer to the water too. It's natural, isn't it? We come from water. Nothing else is so healing.

Still, I lag behind, watching them make their slow, laborious, tender way. Then Andrew is beside me, his hand clapped hard on my back. "Sarah! Didn't you hear me calling? We're going."

The ocean, even though it seems far off, keeps up a deafening roar. "Sorry! Where are we going? Isn't this something?"

"We can't stay here. Our room is no longer available."

"Don't you have the confirmation?" That's probably the wrong thing to say.

"Of course. The manager doesn't give a shit. Her colleague gave our room yesterday to two professors, who come here every year. She says they'll put us in another room. She showed it to me. It's a closet. It faces a wall."

I tell him I don't mind. It's only one night. I'm sure it will be fine. Besides, dinner will be good. We came for that, too.

"I've lost my appetite. *Really*. They say Americans are bad? The French are much worse." He turns toward the stairs. "Are you coming or not?"

His voice cracks in the wind but I'm looking elsewhere. Pools of water are soaking my feet. I don't know if I feel it first, or hear it first, or simply see it. Everything is happening at once. The sea is higher, closer, rushing at us, at them. The man with the wheelchair yells. "Help me. Please help me."

"Andrew!" He is walking away. "Please turn around. Please."

He turns and finally, sees. Peels off his running shoes and socks. We race toward the couple. The man is soaked, and so is she.

Andrew and the man lift the woman off the chair together, blankets and all. They struggle with her up the beach. Andrew calls out, an afterthought, "bring the chair."

Like it's nothing.

The chair is heavy and cumbersome, made heavier with wet sand; the wheels catch. I grip the metal with freezing, slippery hands.

In years ahead, Andrew will tell this story. Always, he will be the hero. Always he will tell how he saved the woman. He won't recall, much less mention, the chair.

I will sit tight-lipped, remembering the icy water lashing my legs as I grappled with the wheelchair. Pretending, as I did then, that it's nothing. Pretending I'm not afraid. Pretending that if it gets too bad, I can simply leave it behind.

Hal's Sleep Showroom

We took the subway to Hal's Sleep Showroom after work. I nudged Cliff to notice the advertisements for Casper Mattresses above the seats. In one, a golden retriever reclined on a queen-sized bed, right ear flopped over. In another, a thumb-sucking child in footed pj's snuggled between her parents, the mattress a king. *Room enough for three*, read the caption.

We had no dog and no child. Although married fifteen years, our mattress needs were modest. We started life together on a waterbed; then upgraded to a Tempurpedic knockoff. By the time that wore out, the mattress world had changed.

"We can't go on this way." Cliff stared at the ads. "Buying mattresses without seeing them first."

"That's why we're going to Hal's."

"Pointless, I'm sure."

Hal's glass-fronted Sleep Showroom was in a white-brick building on the Bowery, wedged between a community center and a lighting store.

"Wait," I said. "Let's not mention our history." Three mattresses, one after another, in a year: *Casper, Purple, Layla.* Emails sent the last day of the trial period.

"*Agreed.* It's private." Our near-perfect timing. Rejects picked up in the a.m.; newbies delivered the same night. We were preparing to shed our fourth: *Bear.*

At 7:38, we were Hal's only customers.

"Glad you made it. You've got 22 minutes to find your perfect night." Hal explained he didn't *sell* mattresses but displayed all the online offerings. You could lie down on them before ordering. If you used Hal's secret code, the manufacturer provided a discount – plus the risk-free 100-day trial period applied. *No questions asked.*

"Sounds good," we said in unison.

Our emails initiating the returns always began *alas*.

Despite website promises, the mattress companies invariably asked: *why*?

It's a hard question, *why*.

We wanted to be truthful.

Was there an online mattress company exchange where they compared notes, figured out who the repeaters were, the ones who were never satisfied?

In fact, no one checked, no one stopped us.

At some point we had concluded that the plushest, firmest, coolest, best-in-class, pressure-relieving mattress would help. At least we would choose *something*.

Hal gave us paper towels to place under our heads and paper booties. He suggested *Bear, Plushbed, Leesa*. Twenty minutes later he announced closing time. We could return the next day. No pressure. "It's a big decision."

That's what our adoption counselor said too, refusing to judge us, though finally she didn't call us back. Three girls, one after another, in three years: Olga, 5; Chen, 7; Angeline, 9. After initial missteps (we weren't religious enough, or of the wrong religion; we were too old; our apartment wasn't large enough; our finances in question), we finally consulted the counselor. Hours had been spent (mostly by me) staring at books of photographs. One of us had fallen in love. The time had come to tell her, then go meet her (for we always asked for a girl). And Cliff would say, *I can't. I know you can but I'm not ready*. Or *it's been too long, I can't anymore*. To our knowledge, the agencies stopped short of telling any of the children, raising her hopes. At least we asked them not to. That is the only kind thing we did. The only expectations raised were my own and theirs: the social workers, the interviewers, the other families we met, the ones who had adopted and were grateful, joyful, filled with good advice and encouragement.

Inevitably as we were on the cusp of saying yes, when we had purchased the airline tickets and had the home inspections, the articles about adoptions that went awry would show up in my inbox. The child was violent or didn't get along with others or had a hidden disease, or in one terrible case killed himself a few years after adoption, believing (wrongly) he had failed to meet his adoptive family's unspoken expectations.

I had continued to hope.

Now I headed for the bathroom, which was in the basement, reached by steep metal stairs.

Just outside the bathroom, a giant poster leaned against a wall, like a door off its hinge. WHEN IS IT TIME TO GET A NEW MATTRESS? Some fool, some miscreant with a neon- blue Sharpie, had xx'd out mattress, substituting mistress throughout:

1) The mistress shows signs of wear.
2) The mistress is sagging or in tears.
3) You are sleeping better with other mistresses, like in a hotel.
4) The mistress offers little comfort or support.

I knew Cliff wasn't sleeping with secret mistresses in hotels. For one thing, he didn't travel much. He had cashed in our tickets to Poland and to China, the ones to Tennessee.

I ascended the stairs, heavy-footed, even in paper booties.

Upstairs, Hal was explaining that he couldn't possibly let us stay the night (an idea Cliff never discussed with me); insurance wouldn't allow it. Cliff argued that an overnight would help us choose. They jousted; I remained silent. Finally, Hal agreed we could stay an extra hour (locked in) while he ran an errand. When he returned at 9 p.m., we would leave; he would close up shop.

After Hal left, I looked at Cliff. What was he thinking? He murmured, *What about this one*? An organic mattress called *Avocado. Firm but pliant.* I shrugged a *why not*? We began on our backs, arms touching. It felt good.

After Cliff fell asleep, I gently extricated myself from his arms. A clear plastic pocket containing a brochure dangled from the Avocado mattress. It depicted a lamb with bedroom eyes.

Cliff lay on his side. I knelt down to look at the brochure.

I read aloud, to no one: "The sheep enjoy getting sheared; otherwise, their coats weigh them down."

I kept speaking softly: a story about a sheep and the benefactor who traveled across the years and across the miles in search of her, who went through many trials before arriving at the right place, who finally found her, who chose her after all.

So Gentle You Don't Feel It

The boarding school in Surrey where Luke taught science gave him the worst bullies to tame. I guess they figured his height (6'4") gave him authority, while his gentle demeanor proved a bloke could be manly without being mean. Luke had the befuddled aura of an absent-minded professor, but his grip could crush you, and he was fierce on the squash court. They said he could separate two tussling sixth-formers with one hand behind his back. Where did that rumor start?

The school knew nothing of Luke's deception. We weren't married, which would have disqualified us from a campus apartment. When I worried he'd lose his job if they found out, he shrugged. "There's no one to tell on us. Besides, we're as good as married." He leaned over, kissed my forehead, tousled my hair. We'd been together three years. My friends in the solicitor's office where I worked knew our status but were too preoccupied with babies and nappies to care. They weren't likely to visit, much less out us.

The school authorities hadn't learned to read Luke the way I did. When we first met, I thought Luke was unattached but soon realized my belief arose not from anything he said but from my own ill-founded expectations. By the time we arrived in Surrey, we had already put that past behind us. We'd sit in the empty dining hall after the boarders were in bed, and he would tell some story designed to make me laugh, trying to quell my fears about the future. The dining hall resembled a medieval Great Hall, but the trappings were fake. The grandfather clock hadn't worked in decades, and the stuffed head of a deer that hung above it had eyes of glass. Luke despised blood sport and often bemoaned the death of that poor stag.

One fine spring night, I intercepted Luke returning near midnight with Anne, the pretty music teacher. He carried a blanket. Their faces were flushed, eyes bright. She murmured goodnight and scurried off. "Wait till you hear what happened," he said. "You won't believe it." He drew me into the dining hall. "Let's sit at the High Table," he said, and snuggled next to me on a massive throne-like chair at its head.

Luke said he'd taken ten boys on a biology field trip that afternoon, to an area where trees were dying from Dutch elm disease. "One young sapling, fifteen feet high, was thriving, bucking the odds. Two boys took their penknives and stripped its bark off. I caught them red-handed." His voice cracked. "I was furious. They took something living and destroyed it, senselessly."

He gripped my hand. I imagined I could feel his heart beating. My own pounded painfully.

"On the walk back," he continued, "the smallest boy, Peter, asked, 'Sir, would it help if we brought a blanket and covered the tree?' He was practically crying. I said 'Perhaps' and left it at that. Then when I was doing evening rounds Peter wasn't in his bed, and his blanket was gone. I went looking; Anne came, too. We found him, sent him home. Here's his blanket."

He draped the blanket around my shoulders like a shawl. It was dark green and rough and smelled of boy. Didn't a story delivered in such even, careful, hushed tones have to be true? Except his eyes kept flitting away from mine to that ancient clock, its hands perpetually at midnight; to the antlers; to the dark sorrowful eyes of that deer.

Ecosystem

Miles showed up out of the blue, begging to camp out in the "den" (once we thought it would be the nursery) before boarding a flight to Istanbul. "That's chutzpah," my mother said. "How long since you heard from him? Two years?" I didn't tell her that Miles brought along his latest floozabelle, an accountant named Megan. "You gave him Samantha Starr Pinot Noir?" My mother was outraged. "Rat poison, that's what he deserves."

She won't acknowledge Miles' strengths. Tall and lean, he projects an aura of concerned sweetness. Back then he lavished praise on my minor, fleeting beauty: pale skin, lank red hair ("soft as a baby's" he said once), small bones. "I hope it takes after you if it's a girl, and after me if it's a boy," he said, before the first miscarriage, and the second. One disappointment engendered another. Even our senses of humor diverged. Suddenly, he was watching Abbott and Costello and The Three Stooges. I'm a David Sedaris fan.

"How's your mother?" Miles asked. Without waiting for an answer, he asked what sights they should visit during their eight-hour layover. Planetarium or MOMA? Katz's Deli or Sammy's Roumanian? He spoke as if he'd never lived here. Conservatory Garden or Cloisters?

"You decide," I said. Megan sat primly on the edge of the sofa, gripping her wineglass in both hands. "Thanks for having us," she kept repeating, as if she had anything to do with it. Her discomfort was a consolation.

More consolation came later: a delivery from the Natural History Museum. I didn't know Megan's handwriting, but the profusion of exclamation points was a clue.

"Hope you enjoy this! Have a good year! Thank you!" and then "M and M!" I doubted M and M would last.

Then I opened my present. The snow globe's defects were manifold.

Here was no village with gingerbread houses and fir trees. Here was only a sticklike tree, gravel, shreds of green, specks of orange like fallen leaves. Half the water gone. A reject. My mother would roar with revenge.

On the printed insert I searched for language about returning defective merchandise. Instead, I read: "When you unpack your EcoSphere check that none of the shrimp are under the gravel by gently rolling it from side to side. Don't panic . . . When the temperature is cooler the shrimp's metabolism slows and they may appear lifeless."

Shrimp? Lifeless? I peered into the globe and held it very still. There was movement there – a flutter. I warmed it with my hands.

It turns out there are three. The insert says these shrimps were selected because they don't display aggression. They are not expected to reproduce.

In my thank-you note, I boasted I could tell them apart – one has longer tendrils than the others, and I've named him Curly. The other shrimp, natch, are Moe and Larry.

I count them each night to make sure they're still there.

Learning to Dive in Bonaire

On my first vacation after the divorce, I learned to scuba dive. Hubert, the hotel's curly-haired dive master, instructed me for a week. I ate alone, studied the manual, sent a postcard of silvery barracuda to my son Theo. "I swam with them today," I wrote, hoping to impress 7-year-old Theo and my ex.

On my next-to-last morning, Hubert offered me a shore dive that wasn't part of the course. We descended, holding hands, among brilliant angelfish and waving ferns. A blue-spotted cornetfish, rare and prized, circled and vanished. Then, from nowhere, a boy. Floating, face down, swimsuit snagged on arms of fire coral.

I tried to stay calm, the diver's first rule. My eyes locked with Hubert's. We ascended together.

"Tell Katya! I'll stay."

My flippers propelled me toward shore. I spotted Katya, head of diving, beside a teen-aged girl. I'd seen the girl before, exhorting her brother to get out of the pool. He reminded me of Theo.

The boy had been missing three hours.

Hubert found me that evening. "Don't eat alone," he said. "Not tonight." He explained how each parent thought the boy was with the other. The girl went snorkeling and her brother tried to follow. While he spoke, Hubert heaped my plate with Island specialties: goat stew I wouldn't touch, roasted papaya, lemony rice.

He taught me words in Papiamento: *beautiful, hot.*

New guests arrived, grabbed rum punches, admired the sea. They ignored the arid landscape.

All Bonaire's beauties are underwater, the guidebook said.

The temptation not to sleep alone was great. But I couldn't say yes to Hubert.

We had held hands that morning as we swam the reef. The boy's hair lifted with the current, peaceful as a fern.

So peaceful I reached out to touch him, as if he were mine.

Reading, Writing, Arithmetic

Reading. "Who will be our donkey?" asked Mrs Lloyd. Third grade. Lance yanked Carly's arm in the air, practically wrenching it out of the socket. Carly kept quiet.

She'd hoped to be a wise man – but was terrified they'd make her the tree.

The donkey costume was from Sarita's father, who had a toy store. Carly couldn't imagine a father who sold toys. Her own father did something important. Since her mother left, he was always angry.

She didn't mind being the donkey. She didn't have to speak.

Writing. In fourth grade, they wore uniforms. Outside for Poetry, Carly sat hunched over, knees to chest. A thick gnarly tree cast its shadow.

Mrs. Conover recited Carly's poem, which she said was the best. "Comments, class?"

"I like pounding rain," offered Sarita.

"I like gashes of lightning," said Jami.

Lance waved furiously. "I like 'trees shake with fear'."

Mrs. Conover said, "I'll turn you all into poets – not just Carly."

But it wasn't Mrs. Conover who taught Carly. He taught pounding. He taught shaking with fear, and what "gash" meant.

Later, Sarita and Jami caught Carly hugging the tree.

"Trees need to breathe!" Sarita scolded.

"I'm not stopping it."

"How do you know?"

Carly knew. She knew you could hug someone so tight they couldn't breathe.The tree wouldn't notice.

Arithmetic. Fifth grade. The year they drew tree diagrams in math. Carly's red pen bled over everything.

The year someone should have put two and two together.

Fathers

We wanted to be fathers. Not ordinary ones who didn't come home because they were working or eating dinner with that other family or because they fought with our mothers and were on a bender. ("What's a bender?" we asked our mothers.) We didn't want to be fathers who lit up in the alley behind the Rite Aid or at the shooting range or at a strip show or at their twentieth viewing of *The Texas Chain Saw Massacre*. We didn't even want to be the fathers who taught us archery at the Fresh Air Camp or whose breath smelled of mint when they leaned over or even the fathers who were math teachers. We already knew (we were told!) we were no good at math because we were only little girls, and we also knew there was something off about us wanting to be fathers and not mothers. We wanted to be fathers like the fathers the girls at the Fresh Air Camp who talked about their fathers talked about. It didn't matter what they said, but it was the way they spoke about them, as if there was a special secret they were sharing.

Above all we wanted to be fathers like the father in the song we learned at Camp around the campfire after someone's father taught us to pile the logs and light the match and toast the marshmallows, gooey and so hot they singed our hands, who taught us to sit next to each other with our arms around each other's shoulders and sway. We wanted to be the father in that song – the song in which the father overhears his little girl in her room at bedtime praying for scarlet ribbons for her hair. We had no hope of being the little girl, whose hair was surely thick and dark and beautiful, not stringy and dirty like ours, and we had no hope of having a father who was out late wandering the streets and despairing because all the stores were closed and shuttered and there were no scarlet ribbons anywhere to be found. But still we wanted to be the father, the father who comes home, saddened by his fruitless journey, peeks in his daughter's room and sees on her pillow "in gay profusion lying there" the scarlet ribbons. Like a mysterious guest.

We wanted to be that father, and if we couldn't be that father, we would settle for being the ribbons.

Hide-and-Seek

When the doorbell rang, Nicky hid in the closet. He imagined his father asking, "Where's Nick-o?" and his mother saying, "I've looked everywhere!" Then she'd leave and his father would come looking for him.

Being found was the most fun, especially being found by him. His mother's dresses shielded Nicky from view; their brushy skirts tickled his face. He waited but his father didn't come. Eventually Nicky crept out of the closet and into the living room. His father stretched on the sofa, talking on the phone.

"I'm using the land line," his father said. "She left. I can't come tonight. Of course I do. Just talking to you I get hard."

When he saw Nicky, he motioned for Nicky to sit beside him. He held the receiver in the air, making squawking motions with his other hand, as if a big bird was talking to him. "Okay," his father said. "Of course, together. Twenty minutes. We'll get ice cream," he winked at Nicky, "and we'll be there."

Heading down Broadway, Nicky protested, "Too fast!" And then: "Baskin-Robbins is the other way!"

"We're getting grown-up ice cream tonight, Nick-o. Sedutto's." He lifted Nicky onto his shoulders. "There you go," he said.

The ice cream store was filled with grown-ups. Nicky expected a kiddie cone, vanilla-fudge, but his father ordered a pint, "half fudge ripple, half rum raisin."

His father walked even faster now. Nicky wondered if they were going to his father's second house, where his father lived without

Nicky and his mother. Then, from high on his perch, he saw something wonderful: a white horse with a red plume, its mane and tail tossing, pulled a carriage down Ninth Avenue. "There's a horse!" Nicky shouted.

Although he and his mother visited the horses outside Central Park, those horses just stood there, waiting for people to pay an arm-and-a-leg for a ride. "It's for tourists,"said his mother. One black horse named Maggie was their friend. They'd bring carrots and if Maggie's driver asked Maggie if she wanted a carrot or if her name was Maggie, she nodded yes. Close up, even Maggie was scary when she went for the carrot. Nicky's mother fed her in the end.

Suddenly his father put Nicky down. "Got stairs to go. Can't pull the back out now, can we?" He pressed a buzzer. "It's Peter and Nick." The lobby was dark and smelled of fish. Nicky trudged upstairs behind his father, wishing he were back home, or on the way home, licking his kiddie cone.

The woman who greeted them wore jeans and a white shirt, her feet bare, toes painted dark red. "Finally," she said.

Something brushed against Nicky's legs and he clung to his father. "You're not afraid of a kitty, are you?" She scooped up a cat, who began meowing loudly. "This is Talbot. Isn't he sweet? I'm Annie."

"Let's have ice cream," said his father.

Nicky couldn't decide if grown-up ice cream was better than Baskin-Robbins. "Is there a cone?" he asked. "Please."

"Only for coffee," she said. "He's cute. Like dad."

"It's warm in here," his father said.

"Yeah, heat on full blast in May. Air-conditioner's in the closet – maybe next time you'll help install it."

She went to the window in the living room, which was slightly open, and opened it a bit more. "I can't open it beyond that or Talbot will go right out."

"You shouldn't," his father said. "Not with Nicky here. No window guards."

"I didn't think of that." She massaged his father's shoulders.

"I could be giving my son a complex."

"That's only when Mommy and Daddy do it. Nick, will you watch TV with Talbot? There's a show about cats of the wild. We'll be in the other room."

Nicky settled in front of the TV, his mouth slick and sweet with ice cream. But watching TV with Talbot wasn't great. Although Talbot looked meek, the cats on the show didn't. Suddenly, Talbot started streaking around the room. His body got longer. His face got narrower. He wasn't a cute kitty any more.

Nicky went and stood by the bedroom door. He turned the knob but it was locked. "Daddy?" he called. Talbot hunkered beside Nicky and began scratching. "Go away!" Annie said. Nicky stood by the window. That's when he saw the horse and carriage standing at the light. Only this time the horse was Maggie.

"Maggie" he called but she didn't hear. He took his two hands, put them under the window, and pushed up. Talbot poked his narrow face through the window, shoulders straining between ledge and frame. "Maggie," Nicky called louder. The light changed and the horse began trotting. "Maggie," he cried with all his strength.

"Nicky," his father yelled, "get away from there." His father was shirtless and barefoot, followed by Annie, in a towel. Annie shouted, "Are you crazy? Talbot could be killed." Talbot had squeezed most of his body out the window. Annie grabbed his squirming fur and hauled him back in.

"You're a bad boy," she said to Nicky.

"Annie! He's three. This was a bad idea. But he's not a bad boy."

"I'm three-and-three-quarters!" Nicky began crying. His father disappeared and came back dressed. He scooped up Nicky – like Annie had scooped up Talbot before – and carried him out the door and down the stairs.

When they arrived home his mother took him in her arms.

"We tried new ice cream," his father said. "The walk knocked him out."

Nicky was too tired to protest. There were things his father hadn't said, things about Annie and Talbot and Maggie.

"I'll tell her tomorrow," he thought.

But in the morning it all seemed like a dream.

"There were horses," he told his mother. "And wild cats."

"Really?" his mother asked. "Wild ones?"

Foley Square, July 2019

The cop asked Feigel to show ID, open her backpack. Clothing, washcloth and towel, her dog-eared copy of *A Long Walk to Water*. Three Cokes in a paper bag, ice-cold, from the deli.

"What are you doing here?" the cop asked. His eyes skittered to the courthouse steps. A crowd was gathering. "Why aren't you in school?"

"My dad's meeting me." She saw him considering whether to believe her. He was sandy-haired, young, not mean-looking. She didn't mention that school was out.

"Not a good place to be, today."

Her father had telephoned for her 14th birthday. He spoke of a new city, a new job at a swanky hotel bar. His place had a bedroom for him and a sofa bed for her, plus her own closet. A bus to the Middle School stopped outside his door.

For the first time she could remember, her father seemed to have thought of everything. How could she say no? It might not happen again.

He said to meet him at Foley Square. "The subway stairs, opposite the courthouses." She could hear him breathing, working his mouth like he did when he was nervous. "Don't tell mom."

When she didn't respond, he said: "Promise."

People emerged from the subway with signs and banners.

Teen-aged girls drew chalk figures on the sidewalk: people killed by cops.

"I can't breathe," Eric Garner had said but the policeman choked him anyway. The Justice Department refused to prosecute.

"Fire Pantaleo!" Eric's mother cried through a megaphone. "You have the power."

Feigel wanted to join them, show she cared. But her father had said "by the subway entrance." He wouldn't want the attention of any cops.

Night fell. The demonstrators went home.

Feigel left her post for fifteen minutes, to use the toilet in the deli.

She always wondered if that's when he came.

Clementine

I told Shannon my Clementine dream: how she's living with a family in Queens.

"You're crazy, girl. Go ask your mom. Your dog is dead. Nobody came to get her. Not an ugly mutt like that."

"She's not ugly," I said. "Somebody adopted her for sure."

"You and your mom killed her – for fifteen dollars a month. That's what everybody says. Rodney kept his boa. Jeanie got her cats. They pay the extra rent. But your mom – she was looking for an excuse, and the Projects Rental Office, they gave her one."

"You're wrong. My mother loves Clementine. "

Shannon claps once and flings open her hands. "Poof! Dead and gone. And not even buried nice. Incinerated."

I don't tell Shannon that Mother said my dream about Clementine is nonsense, too. She never said Clementine was dead, though. "People can control their dreams, Keira," Mama said. "Same way they control themselves at school. People can even control whether they have dreams."

When we eat now, Mother doesn't sit still. She's always hopping up to wash something. Clementine used to lick any dish clean and my mom would only suds them up later. She'd watch Clementine. "Your father isn't good for much, but he picked a good dog."

The last thing my dad did was bring that dog. "Here's Clem," he said. "Present for graduating top of the fifth grade."

"That's no Clem," Mother said, giving the dog a once over. "That's Clementine, you fool." But once he left, once we knew he wasn't coming back, she didn't call Clementine anything but "that dog."

I carried her in a blanket to the ASPCA. I said."Don't be afraid, you're such a nice dog, somebody's gonna choose you right away. Maybe there'll be a girl like me."

The lady at the desk registered Clementine, her name, her age, the date. I heard lots of barking from behind. Maybe those other dogs will be friendly to her, too.

"When you brought your dog, didn't they write the date? That's so they'll know when it's time for her to go to dog heaven. They don't wait long, not with plenty of good-looking dogs around."

Shannon's wrong. Clementine is special. People know, especially some nice family from Queens, with a yard and a swing. I can picture it – like a movie. They walk in and stand in front of her, ignoring the other dogs yapping away. Her one blue eye and one velvet brown fixes that little girl and her father with a look that says, you with me? Even if she barks, they won't mind. Her bark is always "yes" and never "no."

Her whole body wags and she barks "yes, yes, yes!"

Family Day

"Your mother's no good." Angie says. They're on the swings behind the house. Angie's pumping legs are bare from her pink flip-flops to the middle of her thighs where her pink shorts begin, shorts that, she has told Rowena, show off her butt.

It's 80 degrees and sunny but Rowena's wearing a raincoat. It's turquoise, of the same Easter egg intensity as Angie's pink shorts, and too big for Rowena. The swing digs into the back of her knees. She isn't swinging or even sitting, just standing, holding the chains so tight they hurt.

Angie goes on. "Even in jail she's bad. Everyone there's bad, but she's worse. So bad they keep her in a box, built just for her."

Rowena finally speaks. "They don't built no special box just for my mother."

"They have to if she's too fat to fit in the regular one."

Sometimes at school, the other kids are mean and then Angie, small and fierce, defends Rowena. Except for Louise, who they all call Aunt Louise, everyone in this house is like that – nice sometimes and then mean. Even Stevie, who's six, will put his face close to their cat Kiki's face, with her big yellow eyes, talk baby talk to her and then, if she pesters him for food, kick her hard.

The wooden frame house was once white but now the wood shows through brown and splintered. Rowena always gets lots of splinters. When she was little, her mother would sit her down on the toilet seat and drag a chair into the bathroom, banging it against the wall to position it just right. She'd sterilize a needle with a match, hold

Rowena's hand or foot tight, and dig. Rowena would bite her lip to keep from crying. "There. We got the bugger!" Her mother would laugh and Rowena would laugh too, because laughing with her mother was the thing she liked best.

The last time she saw her mother was in the Bedford Hills visiting room on Family Day. Aunt Louise and Roger and Angie and Stevie were all there. She couldn't tell her mother anything. She couldn't tell how when Roger comes home from work sometimes he sits on the edge of the bed and has her rub Ben-Gay into his shoulders and how she can't stop until he says so.

On Family Day her mother wore a bandanna, her eyes glittering snappishly. She asked Rowena for money to buy skittles from the machine. "I'll pay you back, Kit-Kat," she said. "Kit-Kat" was her mother's pet name for her because when she was little, she liked to eat Kit Kat bars. Rowena didn't have any money. She said, "You better ask Louise or Roger."

"Over my dead body," her mother said.

"Next time I'll bring money," Rowena whispered. Her mother said there wouldn't be a next time. She'd be out soon.

The screen door to the swings never closes right. "You let Kiki out!" Angie yells. "She's not allowed in the garden. She'll kill a bird."

"This isn't even a real garden," Rowena says. "There's no birds." But she lets the swing go and walks toward Kiki.

The tabby stares. Rowena imagines Kiki, if she could talk, would be a witness to Angie's meanness, to the thick skin of Roger's shoulders, even to the painful splinters Rowena ignores now.

Kiki arches her back and puffs up her tail. Rowena hears, but doesn't see, a bird chattering in raspy tones, tormenting Kiki. "Pick her up!" Angie orders. "Quick. She's gonna pounce real bad!"

Rowena grabs the squirming fur. Kiki's claws rip the front of her raincoat. "No, Kiki!" Rowena yells, and throws her down. Rowena's raincoat has two long tears down the front.

"I'm telling Aunt Louise," Angie yells. "You threw Kiki! She'll make you go. She'll make you go find your mother, who's out of jail two months already and hasn't even come to see you."

"That's not true!" But Rowena knows it is. Otherwise, how could her mother have sent the raincoat? She couldn't get it inside. There was a card with it: "Dear Rowena: April showers bring May flowers. See you in May. Your Mother."

Now it's June already.

Now the raincoat is ruined, and Kiki, her one true friend, lies at her feet, no longer mewing, just looking at her, not understanding a thing.

No Offense

No offense, Mr. Richards, but saying you have to let me go for lying, that's a lie too. "Letting me go" makes it sound like I wanna go. Bedford Hills, now, they let me go, right through that door I went and never looked back. But you're making me go. And for what? You wouldn't have hired me if you knew about Bedford? But Bedford was only three years out of twenty-seven. For the other twenty-four years I was just like you, walking round, eating pizza, eating lots of pizza to judge by the 250 pounds I got on me. But let's face it, that's why you hired me, scare the customers a little, keep 'em in line. I'm good at this job. I show up every day. I'm even nice to them. I'm big but I can be real soft-spoken. "How can I help you?" "Anything else, sir?" Matches? Straws? I don't forget. Always call a lady miss, even if she's sixty. My momma said to me, "Carla, you're big. You can't be both big and loud. One or the other, you can get by. But not both." She tried to beat it out of me, my loudness, my badness when I was a kid. Always causing a disturbance. The Board of Ed sent me to Special Ed, gave me Thorazine. Momma didn't like that. She'd rather beat me. But I needed the drug sometimes. A nice lady doctor at school, she gave it to me when I said I needed it, and sometimes when I didn't know I needed it.

Me telling you a fake name – that ain't so bad. What's in a name, anyway? And the one I told you isn't so different. You got Carla and Carol, Ward and Word. I happen to like Carol Word better. At Bedford, after my cousin, whose name really was Carol, had passed, this old Jewish guy came to see me and said how a person has two names, the name they get when they're born, and the name they get when they die, that they've earned. Maybe it's the one the angels know or something. Well, I figure I earned another name after three years in the Box. I earned it, to be Carol. Same way I curl my hair now and didn't before, and started wearing nail polish and stopped wearing bandannas.

Bottom line, Mr. R: you know better than some snitching ex-prisoner who waltzes in here by chance one day what goes down. At Bedford we called her "Woody Woodpecker" cause she was always pecking around the dirt for something to use against someone. When she showed up yesterday and asked me, "You got your daughter here somewheres, Carla Ward? The one they took away?" she was trying to make me knock her down. And you said, nice as pie, "I didn't know you had a daughter. That's nice. What's her name?" And when I said "Rowena," you asked, "How old is she?" You didn't blink or say anything bad.

So Woody tried again: "You miss Bedford Hills, Carla? You miss the Box?" She was only in the Box twice – a real Teacher's Pet. I was never Teacher's Pet. Only one who liked me was that lady doctor back at school. She'd tell me magic words to say when I was losing it, make me look them up. Words like "lavender" and "haze." Words like "column" and "quench" and "fragrant." She didn't preach – good, bad, right, wrong. I heard enough from everyone else how bad I was, about the wrong I done. Instead, she gave me them words and tried to get me to hang onto them when things got rough. It was a fine idea. It just didn't work at the time.

Those words come back when I was in the Box, late at night. The Box is solid cement all around, with a feed slot so they can give you your meals and your meds. At night it's real quiet because the other prisoners had their nighttime meds, I had my meds, and the yelling and screaming and banging was over. Sometimes I tried to read a book, and sometimes I thought about them magic words.

When I first came out, I sat in a room in the dark. My other cousin, Carol's sister, the one who took me in, says, "Carla, you got to go out. You got to do something." To somebody else the gas pump is just a gas pump, the broom to sweep with just a broom, the glass panes you look through at the sky ain't worth noticing, the shelves with everything all neat and nice don't mean nothing. But when I cross the road to put garbage in the dumpsters and smoke my cigarette, and look back at them gas pumps shining in the sun, early morning pink haze all round, light glinting off the glass, it looks like paradise. The smell of gasoline is lavender and rose petals all in one. Even how the numbers jump when folks fill up, is like magic. To smoke cigarettes on break, that's magic, too. Inside, cigs is the only pleasure and you gotta do it on the sly. You give some of them girls their cigarettes, leave 'em alone, they might even stop cutting. But Bedford never figured that out. Or they figured it out and didn't care.

You care, Mr. Richards, I know that. You, Mister R – you're my Mister Rehab, Mister Redemption, Mister Rent, Mister Get-My- Daughter Rowena back. You're all that. But you don't let me work here, you don't let me do this, I gotta express it somehow, I'm gonna incinerate like some overheated engine.

Folks with nothing to do – they turn crazy. Nah, I ain't threatening nobody, especially not you.

Ski In/Ski Out

Because she vowed never to become a mother who said "because I say so" and because 15-year-old Nick argued constantly, and because that day in 1999 in Philadelphia it was about a ski trip to Whistler, British Columbia, and how he would never forgive her if she didn't say yes, and because his friends' parents all agreed their boys could go during the February break with two 19-year-old chaperones, and because she feared moguls and icy roads and the boys' collective judgment (or non-judgment), and because she foolishly mentioned avalanches, and because he smirked, "why not landslides, ma?" and stomped out, and because she wondered if she was unreasonable given he'd stopped smoking and was getting A's, which had earned him a direct phone line, including his own beige plastic wall phone, and because it started ringing and he wasn't there, and because, as her ex- said, she and Nick sounded interchangeable on the phone, when she said "hello!" a voice replied, "Nicky! It's Brad. I'm in town, Holiday Inn on Walnut. Can we get together again?" and because this wasn't a 15-year-old voice or a 19-year-old voice but a 35- or 40-year-old voice, she managed, "This is Nick's mother. Who's this?" and because the voice continued pleasantly, "A colleague of his dad's. We met at his dad's place in New Hope," and because her voice unfroze then and she shouted, "Don't ever call him again, ever," and because after that, her heart pounding, she had still promised herself she would never be one to say "because I said so" and because she was certainly not going to be one who said "I told you so," she never told him, or anyone, about the phone call, and because of unrelated reasons, the trip to Whistler didn't happen.

Complicity

It's as simple as this: I needed the apples for my upside-down cake. From the kitchen I peer through the crack between the swinging doors and see the apples nestled in a bowl on the dining room table, fifteen feet from the baby grand. Viktor is at the piano beside 16-year-old Nora, his newest discovery, trying to get her to keep time.

"She goes off somewhere," he complained after last week's lesson. "She has a lovely touch. If she'd learn to count, she could be something."

Normally the living room and dining room are off limits during lessons. Normally I don't get home from work until lessons are done. But I have in mind to make that cake. Two inches of rain predicted. Warm apple cake would be just the thing. Viktor's favorite.

I really needed those apples.

Nora bangs away at the *Revolutionary Etude*, the metronome going like gangbusters. I sneak in from the kitchen, holding onto the swinging doors so they don't whoosh. I avert my eyes. If I don't see them, they won't see me. I grab four golden apples, unblemished, perfect. A dark shadow floats into view: a navy dress folded on the velvet armchair. I look and see Nora's neat rump and curved back on the piano bench beside my husband's tweed-suited backside, his untucked shirt. She wears a white slip, the shoulder straps gossamer ribbons over her pale shoulders.

You ask, why didn't I say something? Clear my throat? Cough? Marvel that girls still wear slips? Weren't they "out" by 1980, when I was 16? Perhaps her dress was tight, impeding the free movement Chopin demands. Or it got wet in the rain and she removed it to dry.

Had the rain even started?

Although placing damp clothing on a velvet chair is careless, it's not a venial sin. I could have mentioned that, I suppose.

What I couldn't do, after two decades of Viktor, was ask, "What the hell is this?" Hear him say, "You're home early, darling. Lessons don't end till six," intimating we'd discuss "this" later. Then he would apologize to Nora for the interruption.

When we married, he was handsome, I was average; he, an artist, I, a paralegal; he, French-Russian; I, from Utica. That first year, after a holiday party, I confronted Viktor. He explained I couldn't possibly have seen what I saw. I was crazy, or drunk. That student wasn't even there, was home with a migraine, an icepack on her neck. I was deeply ashamed.

Viktor, alas, mastered gaslighting along with music.

You say I am complicit. This girl – like the others – was a minor. She needs protection, not me. But what about how small he made me feel, how frivolous my concerns, how baseless my accusations?

On the day of Nora and the *Revolutionary Etude*, I grab my apples and retreat through the swinging doors.

I work fast, too fast: blood drips from a slice on my finger. Quite a lot of blood. I let it swirl into the batter before taping up the finger with a paper towel. The cake is in the oven when the lesson ends and the front door opens and shuts. "Is that apple cake?" Viktor shouts from the living room. "Do I smell apple cake?"

At the Pool Party for My Niece's Graduation from Middle School

I'm a goner even before Leah, my brother's new colleague, tells me her psychiatric specialty ("evaluating sexually dangerous people"), and when she reappears, resplendent in a golden-brown one-piece, I drown in desire. While Leah swims laps, I descend the ladder at the deep end, figuring I can hang on to the side faking it, never letting on I can't swim, my eyes on the prize. Marisa, my niece's best friend, swims up and asks if she can practice life-saving on me; Leah is watching us, and I'm figuring kindness to children is always a plus. But Marisa loses her grip and then I'm grabbing desperately at her orange bikini top and she's yelling. By the time I reach the metal ladder, my coughing subsided, my snotty nose wiped clean, everyone has gone inside for cake. A dead bug floats on the surface, and I wonder who will save me now.

End Game

Our mother wasn't gentle. Party girl, Father called her. She forgave his rages. "You deserve it," she'd tell us, when he grabbed his belt. But all that's old now. Now she can barely speak.

My two brothers absconded years ago. "How is she?" they croak on the phone in alcohol-infused slurs, one on each coast, I in the heartland. I want them to suffer. So I invent a mother they never knew.

"Yesterday she called me 'dear' and 'sweetheart'," I say. I threaten them with good news: "She's improving. We're singing old songs. Having fun."

In truth, I lead. She follows.

"Rudolph the red-nosed rein!" I sing boisterously. She cries, "Dear!"

"Let me call you . . ." I holler. She yells, "Sweetheart!"

"Roll out the barrel, we'll have a barrel of . . ." Silence. I squeeze her fingers. The swollen knuckles, the wedding ring.

"Come on," I mutter, squeezing harder, furious. "Before Nurse gets here."

"Fun!" she screams.

Now You See It

I cannot recall the moment when my relationship with William disappeared. First to go were dinners at a candle-lit table. As the candles burned down, as we spoke about our lives, he might praise my hazel eyes or my shimmering auburn hair. But the day came when his attention moved elsewhere, to my breasts and the smooth silk of my thighs. He lost himself so totally in the pleasures of the flesh that I wondered if he saw me anymore. Except in bed, his expressions of affection were rare. No longer would he grab my hand while we walked down the street. He would sooner kiss the top of his cat Valerie's head, murmuring, "How's the pretty putty-kins," than he would hug me or call me "darling."

It's only a phase, I thought. Be patient. And so I tried. One Saturday morning I sat on his bed wearing only a sheet, waiting for him to finish a business call in the other room, wondering about our future. I stared into the faces of William's ancestors, whose photographs hung over his bed: a stern-looking man, his father, in one photo, and his mother and aunt, wearing flowered dresses, in the other. I didn't like having them eyeing me – members of a family it seemed I would never join. William's bed had a heavy wooden headboard like a ship's prow and was high enough, so I (being small) could have crawled underneath it. Impulsively I lifted the two framed photographs off their hooks and slipped them under the bed, behind the dust ruffle.

William didn't notice anything when he returned. Instead he immediately began caressing me. When it was over, when he disentangled our limbs and went into the bathroom, I reached under the bed to retrieve the photographs and mount them back on the wall. When I couldn't reach them, I got on the floor and peered behind the dust ruffle.

They weren't there. I checked both ends of the bed to be sure, running my hands over the dusty floorboards. When William brought in our post-coital coffees, I almost said something. We sat cross-legged on the bed and drank. For a moment I felt the companionability that had eluded us; then Valerie jumped between us and William kissed her silky head. I experienced a horrible surge of jealousy. Before long, William wanted to make love again. He took our half-finished coffees and Valerie into the living room but left behind a teaspoon on the night table. I shoved the spoon under the bed just before he returned.

This time his passion was even greater; my own, ignited by his. Afterwards, while he showered, I looked for the spoon. It too was gone. Soon I experimented with other objects. A torn shoelace; a dried-out pen. Items only disappeared when we made love. When we simply slept or read in bed, they remained there, dusty but intact.

William didn't notice the missing photographs for days. When he finally mentioned it, I professed ignorance. Once when we made love I took a fresh tube of K-Y Jelly and pushed it behind the dust ruffle. It, too, disappeared.

One summer's day, while we sipped wine in the living room, I thought William seemed unusually tender. I waited, hoping he'd tell me he loved simply being with me. "I have to get inside you," he muttered. I got excited then, too, and we stripped off our clothes on the way to the bedroom, forgetting to close the door behind us to keep Valerie out. When she leapt onto the bed and tried to wriggle between us, I growled, "get her off. "William dumped her off the bed. I opened my eyes just in time to see her make a beeline for the dust ruffle. My face pressed into the mattress, I listened for mewing beneath us. For the first time in my life, I faked an orgasm, my voice, almost catlike, ending in a final yelp.

No more Valerie. William speculated that, offended by his rough treatment, she'd gone back into the living room and out the window. William's apartment was only three floors up; no smashed little body was ever found. William comforted himself that Valerie had wandered off and been adopted by another family, who was taking good care of her.

I thought William's grief was something we could share, an emotional bond between us. It didn't happen. William actually said at one point, "Marian, I know you're trying to sympathize, but you can't understand how I felt about her. She's been with me since she was a kitten." He wasn't in the mood for sex or companionship. I moved out in pained silence. William was right. I didn't know how to comfort him. I'd tried to be there for him always, but he only wanted me – only saw me – one way.

I sent flowers but got no response. So it was with some surprise that I answered the phone a month later to find William. "I'm through the mourning process," he said. "I'd love to see you."

I was silent for what seemed a long time but was probably only a minute or two. "Shall we meet for dinner?" I finally asked.

"Actually," he said, "I'd love it if you came over."

I thought about saying no, about shouting at him, about revealing everything in my heart.

Instead, I went to him. He seemed light-hearted; the only sign of his mourning was that he'd lost some weight. He hugged me, bony and hard. "Come," he said. "I even got a fresh tube of K-Y."

Can you blame me if, in the middle of his passion, when he reached for the K-Y, it wasn't there.

"I think I dropped it under the bed," I said.

"Don't worry, darling, I'll get it," were his last words to me before he crawled underneath the dust ruffle.

I have always remembered that "darling" and wondered, sadly, if I misunderstood him after all.

Do You Remember Me?

"You really remember me?" he asked on the phone. "After 25 years?"

"Of course," I said. "From Honors Lit."

He was between jobs, suggested lunch, wanted to discuss the law.

At the restaurant, he lied and said I hadn't changed. I lied too and mouthed the same words about him. He had changed, from a cute sandy-haired kid with a never-ending supply of pot to a jowly sad-eyed fellow in pinstripes. Over salads, we discussed how we both took up law because there was no living in poetry. We spoke about his girl and my boy, both twenty, both named Jamie – how crazy was that? I commiserated because, unlike me, he'd not remarried after divorce and was still brooding about it.

In my purse I had the business card of a friend who placed temp lawyers and another card for someone who hired out-of-work attorneys as paralegals, but I wasn't sure that's what he meant by "I'll take anything right now."

"You really remember me?" he asked again.

I said I remembered we both loved Delmore Schwartz (which made sense for a Jewish girl from Queens but less so for a prep-school Irish-Scots blue-blood). I remembered when six Honors Lit majors got high and played charades. He acted *In Dreams Begin Responsibilities*. I solved it.

He remembered my kindness.

Then his tone changed. "Here's the truth. I spent three years in rehab. My daughter doesn't speak to me since I stopped paying Skidmore tuition. I can't even get an interview with a firm – you're the only person who agreed to meet me. Will I ever work as a lawyer again?"

I said I didn't know.

We sipped coffee. His hand shook and his spoon clattered against a silver dish of vanilla, his nails bitten to the quick.

I grabbed the check, opened my purse, saw the two business cards nestled there. Undisturbed.

I closed my purse. Paid the bill.

"Funny," he said. "About the charades. I'd forgotten that."

Only after we said goodbye and good luck, did I confront myself in a storefront window. Unrecognizable.

The Decision

Had I known even the gentlest creatures do not go gently, I would have done things differently. I wouldn't have said the vet could come here while you slept on your soft new bed. I would have said no, not yet, insisting that you decide, not me. And as unreasonable as my insistence would have been, I am sure you would have done it, signing on the dotted line in your own good time and at the right time, not like me, my signature wobbly and indecipherable. And even though you had never signed a thing before, had only licked the ink of my scribblings or gripped my pen in your fangs or hid it between your paws, all things you were too weak to do that day or not inclined to do that day, you would, I am sure, have done it if you had only known how afterwards I would never get over it. You would have done it for me.

A Bohemian Memoir

Accustomed to loneliness, I wait, gathering dust, in the breakfront. My mistress's memory of me has long since faded. She is attended to now by caregivers. I observe them all–the gentle ones and the not-so-gentle. *Be careful*, I want to cry out. She is fragile, as fragile as glass.

A hand reaches in, lifts me, turns me, puts me back. They're looking for a wine glass to use in the wedding of my mistress's granddaughter. I have heard that the bride and groom will drink from this special glass. I am excited for the first time in months. *Choose me*, I want to say. My mistress loves me best.

When I speak of loneliness, it's because my siblings are gone: three of them broken in a careless moment, one stolen, one borrowed and never returned. Our guardian, a gold-nosed decanter, has been turned into a bud vase. That's why the thought of a new adventure fills me with hope.

They call me Bohemian. But they do not mean I am anti- establishment or unconventional. Rather I am elegant: tinted a roseate glint, with faint etching in a deeper rose all around my girth and a line of gold (faded now, like my mistress) encircling my rim.

I remember my creation: a glowing torch at my birth; a dark-eyed girl gently washing me in a foamy river; a village in Bohemia. I remember the journey with my five siblings and our shapely guardian. I remember a dark hold, and then an unveiling into the light: a gift for my mistress's wedding.

In my youth, I was used, once a year, in a unique celebration. My mistress filled me with sweet wine and placed me at the center of a long dining table. After hours of eating and singing, all attention focused on me. My mistress told the children about the prophet Elijah, invisible as air, who would visit and drink from my bowl.

A door opened; a cool breeze stirred the surface of my liquid.

From time to time, my mistress used a different glass for the honor at that annual feast. In those years, when she reached into the breakfront for one of my siblings, or even – a time I will never forget – elevated a water glass to the place of honor, there was something pressing on her mind that distracted her. It happened the first time after her daughter, Alice, left for Japan, never to return, and again after her granddaughter, Stacey, broke her leg ice-skating. Each time, the following year, she came back to me. I loved her. I still do.

About a year ago, things changed. It started when her son-in-law, Joel, came to visit on a Sunday afternoon. I recognized the sound of his shoes on the parquet, the leather creaking, the air in the room (usually musty, vaguely perfumed) parting to make way for him: a large man, clumsy but kind. His shadow on the breakfront overwhelmed the dust motes, who disbursed in a flurry of anxiety. "There's nothing to be afraid of," I soothed them. "He means well." Joel complained about the cost of his daughter's upcoming wedding, but in a cheerful way, as if he really didn't mind. "I need a drink," he said, and took me from the breakfront. "Interesting design. Too bad the rest of the set is gone."

He filled me with a caramel-colored liquid, something called (oddly enough) Elijah Craig Bourbon. I hadn't thought about Elijah in months! Was this the same luminary, the prophet? Joel sat beside my mistress, who sipped her peppermint tea. He spoke to her about the plans for her granddaughter's wedding.

"I should live so long," my mistress said. "Can't they move up the date?"

"It's only a year away. You'll be fine. And as beautiful as the bride." What loyalty! Even after his wife Alice – my mistress' daughter – left him and moved far away, to Japan, to become (so I heard) a diplomat's wife, he stayed close to my mistress. After an hour, Joel got up to leave. But he left me on the tray, empty, alongside the bottle of bourbon. Once the front door closed behind him, my mistress picked up the bottle and, with a shaky hand, filled my bowl to the rim. Then she sipped slowly, smacking her lips.

This became our nightly ritual, at 5 p.m. Instead of my being used once a year or on special occasions, my mistress and I spent nearly every evening together. Her caregivers, Rosie and Amelia, discussed it softly during the shift change – whether it was wrong for a 90-year-old lady, who had already suffered a stroke that nearly paralyzed her left side, to drink bourbon every night. She liked to chew a pretzel rod, encrusted with salt, between sips. It wasn't simply the best part of the day for me, but for her as well.

Sometimes after putting my mistress to bed, Amelia would leave me topsy-turvy to dry in the dish drain. Once she put me in the dishwasher and I nearly shattered. Rosie was more careful – the way she was with my mistress. She washed me tenderly at the kitchen sink, rinsed and dried me, and put me back in the breakfront.

If I've given the impression that I'm alone in this breakfront, I must correct it. On the bottom shelf, there are water glasses, stolid and uncomplaining. Then there are the thin champagne glasses, remote and snooty. And in the breakfront's only drawer, folded linen napkins. They too are used for special occasions.

One evening the son-in-law returned. He came in as my mistress had settled in with her bourbon and her pretzel rod. "What's this? The salt isn't good for you, you know that," he said. "And I don't think you should be having alcohol every night when you're taking Plavix and Atorvastatin." He reeled off those names like the internist he was. "Once in a while, but not every night." He meant well, but I don't know. What was the harm? But it wasn't up to us. The caregivers listened to him. And so I went back to my lonely existence.

The caregivers weren't supposed to leave my mistress alone – ever – but sometimes they went downstairs to the lobby, or to walk around the block for some air. The living room felt different when my mistress was alone. I always stood straighter on my shelf when I was in charge of her.

Suddenly the door of the breakfront opened. My mistress' beautiful beaky bird-like face was there, smiling at me. "It's our time," she said. She let go of her walker with one hand and grabbed me. Across the room I saw the bottle on her tray. It seemed so far away. *Don't*, I wanted to say to her. Put me down somewhere, anywhere. You need both hands on the walker, and even then, you are unsteady, you need Rosie to support you. Please, you could . . . but before I could formulate the thought, she fell. She held me aloft even as she went down. When Rosie found her, she was gripping me for dear life.

I'm not sure how Rosie managed to keep it from Joel, but she did. In near hysteria, she called a friend, who called another friend, who sent an off-duty EMT to check on my mistress. My mistress was shaken up, her thin skin was bruised purple, but miraculously her bones were not broken. After a brief period of agitation, her blood pressure returned to normal.

Rosie put me back in the breakfront, in a corner in the back. There was a tiny crack on my rim from my ordeal, but it only bothered me when the weather was bad. For better or for worse, it didn't matter. No one looked at me any longer.

When Joel came the next week to visit, Rosie kept my mistress in her wheelchair covered with a blanket, so he couldn't see the explosion of purplish-red across her chest. He never knew, I'm convinced, he never knew. Even if he had, he was a kind man; he never would have blamed me. I'm sure of it, no matter what happened next.

My mistress went back to sipping peppermint tea in a blue porcelain mug Alice sent from Japan. I remember when the mug arrived, wrapped in red and gold paper, which my mistress folded carefully, saving it to reuse. The mug was tall and stately – like my mistress – and was unusual in that it had a lid with a golden knob in the center. The lid would keep the tea from cooling off between sips. But my mistress didn't like her tea hot. She was always blowing on it and sometimes even dipped an ice cube in the tea to cool it off. Had I the wherewithal to buy my mistress a present I would have known not to buy her that mug. I was not surprised when, the first time she used it, a single tear slid down her cheek. No one else noticed, not Joel, not Stacey, who were both visiting for Mother's Day. But I could tell my mistress was thinking how little her own daughter knew her. Perhaps she wondered whether she would ever see Alice again. And so I learned that there are different kinds of carelessness, but even the most minor kind can cut.

Even though the tea mug caused her pain, my mistress continued to use it. Naturally I thought the mug would come to live with us in the breakfront, but instead, it took its place on an ironing board in a corner of the living room, which in the past doubled as a sideboard when there were enough dinner guests to require it. Now the annual feast had dwindled to just five and the ironing board must have felt itself in limbo, rarely used yet never put away either. Even when the ironing board was used for ironing, say if one of the shy linen napkins needed a once-over, the mug-with-the-lid remained there, sharing space with the spray bottle and the iron, silent amid all the busyness, whether because it couldn't speak our language or because its own nature made it so.

You're probably wondering why I call my mistress simply "mistress" and not her given name, Hazel. I have nothing against the name Hazel, mind you, or any other name. If you asked me, what is your favorite name, your most beloved name, your most exalted name, the most extraordinary name you have ever heard, the answer would be "Hazel." My love of the name – before I even knew there was such a thing as a name – was nurtured from my earliest days in Bohemia, under the shade of a hazel nut tree, which shed its moon-white blossoms on the river of my birth.

Why do people have names? My siblings and I and even my guardian have none; the champagne flutes, in all their superiority, have none; the kindest of napkins have none. I didn't think my mistress needed a name either. Yet from the family's conversations at those annual dinners, I have learned that names have meanings. For example, "Moses" means "to pull out of water" because he, like me, was pulled from the waters of a river. My mistress's name "Hazel" means "God sees." That I can relate to, without even knowing what "God" is. I, too, see the world – in my case, through the glass of the breakfront and sometimes, even through the glass of the television screen. Sometimes, perhaps like God, what I see is too terrible to contemplate. But I am powerless to do anything about it.

Finally the day comes that everyone – my mistress, Joel, and above all, my mistress' granddaughter Stacey, the ice-skater and bride-to-be – has been waiting for. "You made it!" Joel says to my mistress triumphantly as he comes to get her. "You look like a queen." As Rosie gathers my mistress' belongings (her silver-mesh handbag and Pashmina shawl), Joel opens the door to the breakfront and reaches for me. I can hardly believe it! He remembers! He picks me up, runs a soft finger around my rim where the crack is, and sighs deeply. But he doesn't put me back! Instead, he bends and takes an ecru napkin from the breakfront drawer. This napkin is one of the shy ones, folded unto herself. I'm sure she'd rather stay in the drawer. Not me! I am giddy with joy. In addition to the honor of being chosen, I want to watch over my mistress. She rarely goes outside. Who will protect her from the elements?

Everyone's mind (even Joel's, once he has locked the apartment door behind us) is elsewhere.

Something strange happens next. As if to protect me from the elements, while we wait for the elevator, Joel wraps me in the napkin so only my bowl, the depth of my being, remains exposed. I'm confused; how will the bride and groom drink from me?

My mistress, who hasn't left the apartment in nearly a year, is pushed in her wheelchair to the synagogue across the street. Joel carries me and the ecru napkin, locked in a clumsy embrace, in the silk-lined pocket of his dark-blue suit. In the garden adjoining the synagogue, under a peach tree, the guests gather – some fifty in all. My mistress, in her wheelchair, doesn't seem to realize I'm there. She may not even realize she is there. But as Joel removes me and the napkin from his pocket I breathe in the peach-scented air like a tonic. I am immensely happy. The bride is radiant; the groom's face shines like polished glass. Alice has sent a telegram from Japan, which is read so softly, I don't think my mistress hears it.

But then just as the cantor, a young woman, begins chanting, there's some commotion and a middle-aged woman appears whom none of us has seen before. That's what we think at first. But then everyone seems to realize that it's Alice, whom no one – perhaps least of all, Alice herself – expected to attend. She has cut her hair short and died it blue-black with a snowy-white streak in the front and wears a beautiful long silk flowered frock, the same blue as the mug she gave my mistress. She goes to my mistress and puts her hand on her shoulder but my mistress, her eyes filmed over, looks up at this stranger, unseeing. She reaches up her hand, whether to place it atop the stranger's hand or to push the stranger's hand away, I can't tell. But in the middle of the gesture, whether from weakness or a change of heart, my mistress's hand drops back in her lap, her head droops. Am I the only one to see it? I don't see Joel's face, but I feel for him, feel for all of them, at this moment.

The young couple weeps during their vows. Finally, the bearded rabbi, who is surely as ancient as my mistress, looks at her. Her cheeks are etched with a roseate glow, her eyes glint with tears.

"Now, we are almost done. In the midst of joy, we remember sadness, remember this broken world and our obligation to repair it. And so, as at every Jewish wedding ceremony, the groom will break a glass."

Trembling now with fear, I am laid on the ground. How could I have been so blind? The napkin, for her part, comforts me at this moment. She will tell my story, she whispers, holding me close until my trembling stops. But the napkin will be laundered and ironed and returned to a drawer in the breakfront, and the drawer will be closed. Who will watch over my mistress?

I know I will see her again. I will see the dark-eyed girl again, too, with her gentle hands.

The impact is not gentle but a dark shattering static, loud as thunder, followed by shouting – a gabble of voices.

The moment passes. And then, like those annual celebrations, a cool breeze ripples the air, and like my birth, a glowing torch heralds my arrival.

13 Tips for Photographing Your Nephew's Bar Mitzvah When You Still Can't Forgive Your Brother-in-Law

1) Secure your gear. "Shalom! Welcome to B'nai Hayim!" The pony-tailed teen-age usher asks you to leave your camera bag in the cloakroom; photography is forbidden during the service. You promise to hide it under your seat but explain you can't risk losing it. She frowns; who would steal a camera during a Bar Mitzvah? Still, she relents.

2) Prepare for the unexpected. Why did Harry and Sarit turn to you when their professional photographer bailed? You didn't even own a camera until yesterday (a point-and-shoot from B&H, fully refundable). You're pondering this question while the rabbi speaks about punishment and forgiveness in Adam's Torah portion. Do the sinning Israelites have a future? Harry and Sarit sit on velvet-upholstered chairs flanking the rabbi; Adam beams in his blue suit; the seven-year-old twins disrupt the first row, mugging, chatting, ignoring the shushing. They are your secret loves.

3) Capture memories as well as moments. Your sister claims Harry said you were a true memoirist, the best photographer in the family. *Really*? You haven't photographed him in 16 years; blurred black-and-whites, an antique Polaroid. Then again, Harry's standards were always low, his murmured *on your knees, darling*. You push away these thoughts, the reason you see your family only once a year.

4) Consider a collage using old photos. Sixteen years ago. Late afternoon. The sun-dappled foyer of your parents' house in Philly. You and Harry have driven from Ithaca; everyone assumes you connected on Cornell's ride board. Meeting your beautiful older sister Sarit, Harry comments what *good company* you were on the five-hour trip. The months you spent together, the handsome grad student teaching the avid freshman to fellate him just so, your post-coital bodies braided like warm challah, fragrant and glistening with moisture. *Good company.*

5) Anticipate the weather. Outside the shul, thick alabaster clouds, no trace of blue. With an opaque white sky as backdrop, everything increases in intensity; colors flame; emotions flare; rain threatens.

6) Remember to tell a story. Sixteen years ago, leaving the clinic, you focused on a whited out sky, skirting the kneeling women praying for your salvation, taunting: *boy or girl, mama*? At seventeen, you believed the time would come when you would no longer recall that day, much less the softly falling, unforgiving snow.

7) The rule of thirds ("avoid the bullseye"). At the outdoor buffet, you wolf down franks-in-blankets; perhaps your only chance. You circle the tent. Adam, flanked by grandmas, lighting a candle. *Check.* Grandpas, hands joined over the challah. *Check.* Adam, Harry, and Sarit hoisted in chairs, requiring several takes because you keep chopping off Harry's head. *Check.* Adam and the twins: *where are the twins*?

8) Don't leave anyone out. At the kids' table, 12-year-old girls with half-purpled hair vamp in tiny dresses; Adam and his best buds play poker; smears of mustard, chocolate, grandmas' lipstick. You snap them all. You ask Adam if he's seen Josh and Jake. "Sorry, Aunt Leah." Silently begging *please don't make me find them.* At the old people's table, everyone smiles, coffee cups aloft, Sweet & Low packets ripped open or secured, in handbags, against future bitterness. Your grandma, the prettiest of them all, with the bluest eyes (inherited by Sarit and Adam), points to the house. "Harry's punishing them."

9) Let family squabbles run their course. Here, you must disagree. Away from the music and tumult, the house is quiet. Except for Jake. How long has he been crying? An hour? Two? You wrap him in your arms, tell him you love him, that he is the best boy in the world; one day he will know that. You speak to him but also to the one who isn't there, the boy you sometimes think about, though you never confirmed it was a boy. Eventually Jake relaxes, calms in your arms. Josh, pretending nonchalance, looks up from the latest *Redwall.* For weeks they've heard about the candle-lighting, the chairs, the cake. What about their memories? You feel bad for the boys having Harry for a dad.

10) Be bold – go for the shots you want. You hold out your empty hands, the camera dangling from your neck. "I'm sure there's chocolate cake left." Their dark curls are askew; their skinny arms fragile in white short-sleeved dress shirts. Josh murmurs, "but Dad said . . . ." You tell them not to worry about Harry. Outside, the music has died except for a mournful sax playing *Unforgettable*. They race to the empty seats at your grandma's table. She looks at you and understands. Not all of it but enough.

11) Change your perspective. The light has changed, the clouds shifted, a glimmer of rainbow on the horizon suggests it rained nearby. You change the setting on the camera the way the B&H guy showed you. "Where *were* you, Leah?" Sarit asks. She hasn't noticed the twins, not yet. She is not a noticer, your sister. "The Millers' table hasn't been photographed. People are starting to leave." She hesitates. "Thank you for all this. Harry and I owe you big time." You tell her no problem. You tell her you're on it. You don't say you're welcome.

12) Images, even mistakes, can be manipulated. Because you are the photographer, there will be no pictures of you. Is a future even possible in which you reclaim your position in the family, or at least a position? Go from being Aunt Leah on Thanksgiving to something else? Help the boys flout their father's edicts, their mother's cluelessness? And then what?

13) Take a deep breath. You're getting all the tables, the last dance, when you know he's there, Harry, standing behind you. You don't have to turn and look. It's his smell. Dial Soap and Balkan Sobranie and his sweet dark messy hair, which he is lucky at 41 to have in abundance. He is lucky and you say a prayer, your first real prayer of the day, that his boys end up lucky, too.

II
IN THE REPAIR SHOP

Tiffy

My ex-husband bows at the waist before introducing her. "Irene," he says, "this is Tiffy." Pete is 66, a decade older than I, but handsome as ever in his tux. I haven't seen him for over three years but have heard about his escapades through the grapevine, while I spent my evenings with the grapes.

I shake hands with the blonde twenty-something beside him. She's wearing a green-and-black sheath dress and iridescent earrings that gleam like barracuda. Her hand is warm, fingers slender, nail color matched to the earrings.

I can't manage "pleased to meet you" or even a starched, Eliza Doolittle-post-Henry Higgins, "How do you DO?"

"Tiffy," I say. "Unusual." She starts to speak but I interrupt. "I've never met a real-life Tiffy, only the Sesame Street character, back when I worked on the show. Circa 1998. Probably before you were born." That would have made her sixteen, which even I know is wrong.

"Irene-y," Pete says, a familiar warning in his voice. "Irony," he continues, using his pet name for me, from better times. "You're looking lovely. Imagine, mother of the groom!" He glares.

We are at our son Dan's wedding.

I can't stop. "You weren't named after everyone's favorite jewelry store?"

"Not at all," the girl says. She really does have a beautiful smile. "People always ask. But here's my mom. She'll tell you."

Pete reaches out to hug Tiffy's mother. "Irene-y," he says, "I want you to meet Rachel." He hesitates. "My fiancée." Rachel is in green, too, a pale linen pants suit that's stylish but wrinkled. Her face is carefully made up. "Rachel, this is Irene, Dan's mother. She was asking how Tiffy got her name."

"Short for Tiferet," Rachel says. "From the Hebrew for compassion."

Breakfast with Henry

The other driver was looking at her cell phone, you're sure of it, but there's no one to back you up. Henry certainly can't do it, so you hand your license to the police officer, and he asks if you think you can walk a straight line. His partner, a woman whose wavy red hair hangs below her cap, is examining the damage to the other car and speaking with the other driver. You know there is always a good cop and a bad cop and you are hoping you got the good one, but you just don't know. He shows you a card that says you are free to refuse the field sobriety test but that there may be consequences. You want to ask *what consequences* and what if God forbid your license were suspended, but worry about your breath and decide the less said the better. You have had your usual Sunday brunch, two Bloody Mary's and cinnamon toast, and your 60-year-old nephew Henry has had his usual – a vanilla milkshake – plus he's now got all three swizzle sticks from your drinks (three, count 'em, not two), plus the lemon wedges, two of which he has already sucked dry.

Henry has wandered off in the parking lot but not too far; you see him toeing a black shoe in the gravel, and muttering his words: *milkshake, steak, soup, hello, goodbye, catsup,* and *Mommy*! You are not his Mommy but sometimes you say to him that you know he must miss her and he always responds with *Mommy*! and sometimes he weeps. As usual, he is decked out handsomely for your Sunday excursion: jockey cap, herringbone jacket, black chinos, and those leather shoes. The cop asks if your passenger can vouch for you, but you shake your head no, no, he can't and his eyes bounce to Henry and back and he seems to get it.

Maybe he's the good cop.

If you were destined to hit a car today you are glad that you were still in the diner's parking lot, the diner where you come with Henry every

Sunday, picking him up from Camphill Village, where he lives with ten other residents in a group home with a house mother. Henry is the reason you moved to Copake to the one-room walk-up; the reason you left Stuyvesant Town and rent control and your small circle of friends; the reason you said goodbye to your neighbor and sometime lover Cal, who said you were crazy to move to be near Henry, who doesn't even know what an *aunt* is. Whenever you pick up Henry on Sundays, and he hugs you briskly and shouts "shotgun" before settling into the passenger seat, you know Cal is wrong.

Florine, the waitress who knows exactly what you both want even before you sit down, is on her lunch break, having a smoke, watching from just outside the diner's back door. Of course, if the cop really wants to know how much you had to drink, he has only to ask Florine, only to examine the receipt.

You think the best thing you can do is pass this sobriety test with flying colors. You concentrate hard and try not to be distracted by Henry, who has edged closer. The officer draws a chalk line on the tarmac. He reads aloud from another card, which he holds at arm's length, so you can read it too: *You will put your left foot on the line, then your right foot on the line ahead of it, heel to toe. You will take nine pairs of steps. Then turn and come back the same way. When you turn keep your front foot on the line and turn by taking several small steps with the other foot. You MUST look at your feet at all times and keep your arms at your side. DO NOT STOP until you have completed the test.*

His voice changes and he asks: *Do you understand? Do you understand?* You say you do. It is a lot to keep straight but you begin. The hardest thing is to look at your feet, which are flawed and ugly in sandals, the Fujiyama Mama pink polish chipped, your insteps dirty. Unlike Henry's shiny black shoes which you see walking beside you on an imaginary chalk line of his own, mimicking your every step. You can't help it. You take your eyes off your feet. You grin at Henry, starting to laugh, and he grins back. Your arms flail to steady yourself, but you can't stop.

Maybe, just maybe, you got the good cop.

How My Mother Lost Her Voice and Gave Me Mine

In 1931, my mother Helen was nine. A daredevil, she challenged boys at their games, ignored their hair pulling, their scrunchy faces. My grandmother warned: "Act like a lady!"

One day, on roller skates, racing a boy on his bicycle, Helen went flying. She hit her jaw on the pavement, knocked out her front teeth, a blood-soaked mess. The dentist refused to replace the teeth until her mouth "matured." Ashamed of the gap, Helen stopped speaking, brewed silence in her genes like strong tea.

Eventually she turned out one quiet child after another.

Until I showed up, red-faced and bawling.

Eavesdropping

After the yellow roses and the Chablis Premier Cru and the buttery Chilean sea bass (let's forget it's nearly extinct for one night, darling), after the kisses shivering the back of my neck and hands parting my silk robe, after the Thelonious Monk and the robe falling and the taut sheets, and after my hot mouth singeing the soft, bristly, chocolatey hairs of his belly, there is the baby monitor.

"I'll go," I say, pushing myself up with force. The wailing means she's wet. We have learned her different cries, learned them all.

"No, you stay here. I'll go."

I am lying face down uncovered. My ass, when I turn to look at it, is white and round and to him, I know, perfect and complete, a world unto itself, even if I think it's too big. "Whatsa matter, baby?" I hear him over the baby monitor. "Whatsa matter? Daddy's here." There is the noise of velcro ripping and diaper gel oozing. "Oh, what a pretty tushy, what a wet pretty tushy." He begins to sing: "Daddy's gonna dry it, yes I am, Lizzie's gotta diet, chub-wub-ham!"

The wailing stops. "That's a good Lizzie," he croons. When he comes back, I'm on my side with the sheet and quilt over me.

He puts his arms around me from behind. Before Lizzie, there were no yellow roses, no Chablis Premier Cru, no nightgowns, no Monk. Before, there was just us. "You're a prince," I whisper. He massages my shoulders and I feel him rising against my ass, and it's different now, with my back turned, and after his hand drops below my waist, and after he strives against me and after my resistance flags and after our breathing sounds like nothing we've breathed before, there's the baby monitor.

"Shit."

"No," he says. "Not shit; it's the wrong cry." He's right, this is the hungry, stick-your-tit-in-my-face, cry.

"Me," I say. He tries to hold me back, but I slide naked out of bed and run angrily into her room. "All right, all right," I say and take her and sit in the rocker. The wicker is rough against my naked back, but she is warm against my breast and when she sucks hard, it feels better than good.

"Oh," I cry. "Oh. Oh."

Right into the baby monitor.

Susceptible to Scratches

Before the pandemic, the desk had been his province exclusively since only he worked from home, but in their forced togetherness, they had to share it. He bragged about how he and Marnie, his ex-wife, rescued the desk during a snowstorm, when the Northwestern Law School Library replaced its wooden desks with metal ones. Had they not taken it, the desk would have been brought to the town dump, to be scavenged by humans or animals unknown.

The desk was not without flaws. It bore round marks from water glasses and sharp narrow furrows left by pens or protractors. Still, the work area was deep and wide and the legs square and sturdy. The wood was a mix of grains: wavy, herringbone, copper colored, buffed to soft beige in places. It smelled of deep forest and smoke, as dark and unknowable as his life was before they met.

They had been married only a few months when everything changed. Although she liked the desk's woodsy aroma, when she reached inside the sole drawer, she felt grit and dust. The drawer stuck dangerously, suggesting that if one grabbed the chipped knobs too enthusiastically, it might come out altogether. None of that bothered *him*, he didn't even notice, but she wanted to clean the inside. She wanted the drawer to run smoothly on its casters. She found a guide to handling old wood furniture, which recommended *honest and sympathetic treatment*. That gave her hope. She was both honest and sympathetic. The guide's instructions, however, were all about treating the outside of the desk, not the inside. How to avoid spills and wet rings before they became indelible; how regular dusting would prevent airborne particles from leaving a film that could scratch the surface; what type of cloth to use for dusting, cloth diapers being particularly recommended. *Even with the best care, injuries can happen.*

She veered from hope to despair and back again, sometimes multiple times a day. Finally, she dampened paper towels with a mild solution of water and dish detergent and reached in to clean, and then dry, the inside of the drawer. She applied negligible amounts of WD-40 so it rolled effortlessly on its bed. When checking the deep recesses of the drawer for dirt, she found a folded page. It contained no revelations or intimacies exchanged between her husband and his ex, only Northwestern Law Library Rules: patrons should not harass or annoy others; sleeping and eating were prohibited; animals and unattended children would be reported to the County Sheriff. Those instructions had remained, hidden and undisturbed, during the decade of her husband's first marriage.

She had wondered if she would ever feel comfortable using the desk. Now her heart lightened. In truth she had no choice. Besides, there was an engraved "N" on the drawer, for Northwestern, between the two chipped but serviceable knobs. "N" was her initial, not his and not Marnie's.

And so, she laid claim to the desk and to him.

Security Device

"You taking good care of your mother?" Burton Beetle asked at the class picnic. It was a year after my dad died. Beetle, my fifth-grade teacher, was practically drooling over my Mom. Even his mustache looked moist.

But Beetle didn't stand a chance. After two cars were hijacked on Queens Boulevard in one week, Mom ordered a life-size inflatable Safe-T-Man from Hammacher Schlemmer to ride beside her in the front seat.

She knew I'd be mad, stuck in the back. "It's a visual deterrent," she said, reading the catalog. I was a green belt in karate, starting middle school that fall. Why did we need a plastic bodyguard?

"Come help me inflate him, Jerry," Mom said. Clint (I named him) cost $99.95, plus $9.95 for a dual-action inflator pump. Made of highest quality vinyl, he weighed 7 lbs 3 oz.

"Same as you when you were born," Mom said.

Inflated, he resembled a six-foot tackle.

Better Clint than Beetle.

That summer we raced around air-conditioned supermarkets, went to horror movies and the Y pool. Clint waited in the car, double-parked.

In September, with her driving me to middle school, I had to do something. The guys would think she was nuts. I carried him inside, gave him some air, stuck him on the sofa. "What purpose can he possibly serve inside?" Mom asked.

"Let's just try it," I begged.

Now he's there permanently. While I do homework, she sits beside him and reads. I have seen her pat his arm.

Adventureland

Over their last breakfast at the condo in Montauk, Clay told Nicky about a new ride at Adventureland called "Spinning Dinghies," which was just right for boys his age. Clay said he was surprised that Nicky hadn't been to Adventureland in his nearly four years on this earth. "She never took me," Nicky explained matter-of-factly, pointing at Celia.

Clay grinned at Celia and said his own two boys, who were ten and twelve, loved Adventureland when they were Nicky's age.

After that, it was inevitable that they would stop there on their way back to the City. Celia hated amusement parks but didn't want to spoil it for Nicky. Was it the noise, the tinny music, the screaming? The waiting in line? She tried to remember whether she'd had a bad experience at an amusement park as a child, but only recalled feeling overwhelmed. Every so often there was something in the news about a ride that malfunctioned; a Ferris wheel stranded its passengers in mid-air; a roller coaster went off track. She couldn't imagine why anyone wanted to be scared to death. But here they were.

As Nicky raced from the parking lot to the entrance, Clay grabbed Celia for a hug. "I adore you, Ceci," he said, a refrain from the night before when, not for the first time in their three-month relationship, he urged her to give up the one-bedroom rental where she lived with Nicky and move in with him and his boys (who were with their mother half the time) in his co-op on 89th and Park. He urged other things on Celia, too: that she go from five days a week at her firm to four, and get her hair cropped in a Halle Berry-style pixie. "You have the bones for it," he said. "And that lovely curve of neck." More things, too, he offered: private school for Nick, even a therapist to straighten out Nicky's crooked left leg, which required Nicky to wear special orthopedic shoes. But Nicky's orthopedist said that if they waited a year the condition would probably correct itself. In the meantime, Nicky inexplicably adored the clunky white Oxfords as if they were Air Jordans.

Clay couldn't understand Celia's reluctance to accept his largesse. Nor could Celia's best friend, Marta, who said it was about time Celia had a man who treated her and Nicky right, especially after Celia's experience with Nicky's father, Tad. Tad's free lance photographic career not only didn't pay the rent but included cheating on Celia in the marital bed while she was at work and Nicky played in the next room.

When she asked Tad to leave, days before her thirty-seventh birthday, Celia wondered sadly whether she would always be alone. She wondered if she was doing something terrible to Nick, depriving him of his father's daily presence at the tender age of two. Then, at a performance of *As You Like It* at the Delacorte – a rare night out, with tickets Marta won in the on-line lottery – there was Clay squeezing past them to get to his seat. "Don't get up," he said gallantly. Celia couldn't believe that less than two years after parting from Tad, someone as kind, smart, and, as Marta put it, "fucking rolling in it," wanted to be with her. With *them*.

"He's one in a million," Marta said, when she met Celia for drinks two months after the evening they met Clay. Marta was pleased that it was her winning the Shakespeare-in-the-Park lottery that had brought Celia and Clay together. Both Celia and Marta worked full time; if they'd had to stand in line for tickets, like most audience members, they'd never have gotten in. Clay had attended with a group from his law firm, which paid some enormous premium not to wait in line at all.

"His boys don't like us," Celia said. "Or at least they don't care for Nicky."

"They don't want to share," Marta said. "But I'm sure they'll get over it." The word that came to Celia's mind was spoiled – a word she didn't want to share even with Marta. Marta would only say, "So what's wrong with being spoiled? It's about time someone spoiled you and Nicky."

Still, Celia cringed when Clay's ten-year-old, Nate, thinking no one was looking, gave Nicky a shove when he got too close to the bicycle wheel Nate was repairing, so that Nicky fell on the gravel driveway. Twelve-year-old Julian was perpetually annoyed because Nicky would swing his feet against the back of Julian's seat when they all piled into the Jaguar. "Dad," he'd say, "Nicky's denting the leather" and would scold Nicky. "Stop that! Stop that now!" To make peace, Celia removed Nicky's shoes on the few occasions when they were in Clay's car together. But the boys continued to complain. Nicky's blonde curls, they said, made him look like a girl. They mocked his clunky white shoes. "Shut up about the shoes," Clay said, although privately to Celia he renewed his offer of muscle therapy to straighten Nicky's chubby legs.

As for the hair, he sided with them. "Nicky needs a haircut. Boys should look like boys."

Celia kept putting it off. "In September," she said. "Before he starts nursery school."

She was relieved that for now the boys were at camp. She wondered vaguely if they got their meanness from Clay, or from their mother, whom she'd never met. Or if she was simply too judgmental. They were children, after all.

"Besides," Marta continued, as if reading Celia's mind, "he's not mean. He not only would give you the shirt off his back, he did." Celia couldn't deny it was true. During Act III of the play, when an unseasonable wind rattled the trees in the Forest of Arden, and Celia wrapped her arms around her bare shoulders, Clay, who had chatted with her during intermission, pulled his grey sweater over his head and silently offered it to her. She tried to refuse. "You must," he insisted. A man in the row in front turned sharply and glared at them for talking. So, Celia put on the sweater of this now T-shirt clad stranger, the soft wool still warm from his body.

Nicky offered less resistance to Clay's charms. Clay made butterscotch pudding for him, as he did for his own boys. A week before the trip to Montauk, when Celia and Nick were getting ready to go to Clay's place for dinner, Clay called Nick on the phone to say he'd put the pudding in the fridge to set. Nick handed the phone to his mother and then came close and whispered in her ear, "I think I love Clay."

Once inside Adventureland's gates, Nicky went right to the carousel. He loved carousels, loved picking his steed and having Celia mount the horse next to his. They'd gone on the carousel in Central Park half a dozen times.

"Can we go, Mommy?" he asked. "Can we?"

"I don't see why not."

"Maybe later," said Clay. When Nicky stood transfixed, Clay added, "Hey, I almost forgot, cotton candy's first on the agenda." He took Nicky by the hand, and they went right up to the pony-tailed girl spinning the cotton candy and bought one, which Nicky practically inhaled.

"Ceci?" Clay asked, but Celia said no.

It didn't take long for Clay and Nicky to find the Spinning Dinghies. The ride had individual rowboats that would spin as they raced in a bumpy circular track over an alligator-infested lagoon. "Mommy, will you come, too?" Nicky asked as soon as he saw it. But Spinning Dinghies had height requirements, minimum (42 inches) and maximum (52). Even in his thick-soled orthopedic shoes, Nicky was too short, just over 40 inches.

"Your mom can't go anyway, buddy," said the man taking the tickets. He had a classic handlebar mustache and a creased, leathery look, like a TV outlaw. "Wait till next year."

Celia was relieved. The other children, who were already strapped in, looked enormous compared to Nicky, at least five- or six-years old. And given Nick's nightmare the previous night, she wasn't sure an alligator-infested lagoon – even a pretend one – was where Nick needed to be right now. She hadn't known how long he'd been calling from his room when she heard him. Gently extricating herself from Clay's arms, she went to him. He had dreamed there was a flying alligator in his room and woke to a loud rushing sound that frightened him even more. She reassured him that there was no alligator, flying or otherwise, only the rustle of curtains from a sharp sea-borne wind, and the louder rush of waves outside his window. He'd never slept by the ocean before. Neither had she.

Now, as she took Nicky's hand to lead him back to the carousel, Clay handed the "Spinning Dinghies" attendant a bill. Celia saw that it was a fifty. The man looked around, sighed, winked at her, and said to Nicky, "Okay, buddy, climb on."

Nicky clambered into the last seat before Celia could stop him. The attendant slipped the fifty in his pocket and strapped Nicky in.

"I can't believe it," Nicky grinned. "Bye, Mommy."

The theme from *Jaws* screamed from the loudspeaker. Nicky, his blonde curls streaming, went flying along the track, the dinghy spinning as it flew. The next time Nicky came around the curve where Celia stood, he was no longer smiling. He looked at her open-mouthed and then disappeared again, flung from side to side in the dinghy, and the third time he came around he was crying, his face a glistening red ball. The other children were screaming. Three more times Nicky spun past, his eyes squeezed shut, his red face streaming with tears, his hands gripping the sides of the dinghy. When the ride ended, he sat, head bowed, crying.

She ran to him, undid the straps, and lifted him out. He clung to her, sobbing, his face wet against her chest. Her own eyes were wet, too, her own heart beating as frantically as his, her own head spinning.

Eventually the feel of Nicky in her arms calmed her.

Clay stood a little way off. When she finally looked at him, he shrugged, a half-smile on his lips.

"Too young," the ticket-taker volunteered. "Should have waited another year."

"Maybe," Clay said. "Still, it was worth a try. Right, buddy?" He walked up to them and swatted playfully at Nicky's calf. "Have to learn to be a man sometime."

Nicky's shoulders stopped heaving.

"I know," he said in a sad, muffled voice.

Celia thought he might start crying again but he didn't. His shoes dug into Celia's thighs.

"Probably we should head home," Clay said and began striding in the direction of the parking lot. Carrying her son, Celia followed.

The night before, after she soothed Nicky back to sleep, she'd gone out onto the terrace. Like Nick, until that weekend, she'd never slept so close to the sea. She stayed on the terrace for an hour. The night was so wonderfully free of human noise, filled only with the sound of the waves.

But now, instead of the ocean, there was the image of Clay handing the attendant a fifty-dollar bill. In her arms, she felt Nicky's weight and knew he'd fallen asleep. Clay had already reached the parking lot and turned to look for them. But she didn't speed up to meet him. Instead, she trudged; the gravel crunched under her sandals. She was grateful for the distance, for her son's heaviness in her arms. It made her slow down.

Marta would want to hear about everything. But words would fail when Celia got to the sound of the ocean, the sound of Nicky's weeping, the sound of Clay starting the engine before they even reached him.

Bar Mitzvah

When Benjy started to choke on a piece of celery stuffed with scallion cream cheese, I turned from the buffet table and asked, are you okay, and when he shook his head, I said raise your arms but he kept choking, so I slapped him on the back of his fancy new suit, and then two words clicked in my head Heimlich maneuver so I punched my fist into his stomach even though this was the wrong way to do it, but I couldn't think, couldn't think of the right way, his gray eyes huge and terrified, I had never seen him that scared, so I cried we need help over here Benjamin is choking and then she was there, Dinah, the wicked stepmother in her fuchsia gown, the airline stewardess (flight attendant, Benjy had corrected me once, don't be sexist, ma) and she clasped her arms around him from behind and jerked back hard and the celery flew across the room on angel's wings and I said thank you God while this woman who had wrecked our lives ten years earlier hugged my son and I knew then, on his Bar Mitzvah day, that for everything there is a purpose under heaven.

Destiny

First his mother sang of piggies and dogies that git along and doggies in windows. Then she called him "Sugar Pie" and it stuck, stuck like spun sugar to his mouth and melted there. Afterwards she called him that often.

When he was six, with curly hair that flopped in his eyes and went halfway to his shoulders, she used the name while chaperoning a class trip to the Planetarium. The other boys crowed: "Sugar Pie! Mommy's Sugar Pie!" After that, she cut his hair and called him by his real name, but he was marked. He fought incessantly after that, never still.

At sixteen, he met Carissa, a delicate bud, allergic to nuts and gluten. For her pleasure, he made a gluten-free crust for his pecan pie, sans pecans. When she tasted the oozy filling, she exclaimed, "Sugar Pie. Like in Montreal. My favorite!"

She took tiny portions of his Sugar Pie on the smallest teaspoon she could find (a serrated one, meant for grapefruit), and made each teaspoon last unbearably long as she teased it with her tongue. Watching her, he could barely breathe.

When Carissa left him, he was inconsolable. Until one night out in Ithaca with a townie named Tamar, both downing lemon drop shots and soured on love, they began trading pet words for their private parts, or, more precisely, the words others had called them. He confessed to Rocky, Seymour, and Oedipus Rex. Tamar said hers had been called Millicent, Mount Etna, and Sugar Pie.

"Sugar Pie?"

She blushed. "I guess it's not very original."

"I don't know," he mused.

He inhaled her scent, a heady mix of sour and sweet. "What's that perfume?" he asked, bringing her hand to his lips. She blushed again. "It's called Destiny."

And he wondered if she, or even they, might be more than he thought.

Spirit of the Staircase

At 7 a.m. Saturday, the side street off the Rue du Temple was quiet. After several minutes, Robert answered her insistent knock. He was in jeans and a T-shirt, rubbing the beginnings of a beard. His long white feet were bare.

Emily told him she was sorry to disturb him but she'd left her flute there the night before. She was sure of it. She needed to get it because she was leaving for New York in four hours. Frankly, she was in a panic.

"I'm afraid it's not here, Em. Come in anyway, though. I'll make us some café. Amazing, seeing you for the second time in 24 hours. After 15 years." The flute wasn't where she thought she left it the night before, on the mahogany table in the foyer. The table was bare except for a lapis blue bowl, filled with clementines. She remembered the bowl from the night before, thinking how well it suited Robert: the deep blue glaze, the bright orange fruit, an attention to detail that was, in the end, pointless. That's how she remembered Robert from 15 years ago, when they were college juniors abroad in Paris. Now she thought that, as young as she was then, she'd been right.

Her decision to go to dinner at Robert's was undeniably foolish – and the missing flute was her just reward. When she got his email after 15 years of silence, she had wondered whether to respond. "I'm playing a recital at Church of the Madeleine, part of their noon-time series," he wrote. "Debussy. I couldn't help thinking of you. So I Googled you and there you were." Remarkably the email arrived ten days before her long-planned business trip to Paris. She wrote back to Robert about her life as a lawyer in New York, about her trip and upcoming marriage. She didn't mention (it hardly seemed important) that her fiancé, Sandy, an amateur flutist ("flautist" he would say), had sent his 10-year-old flute to Paris to be overhauled. Part of her mission in Paris was to retrieve it for him.

"We must get together when you're here," Robert emailed. "For old time's sake."

She told her best friend at work, Renee, about Robert's emails.

"Isn't that the way? You hear from them when it's too late." Renee wore her auburn hair so short it was practically a crewcut. She had freckles, three gold earrings in each ear, and bright blue eyes. She was four years younger than Emily and often said things aloud that Emily only thought.

When Robert emailed that he would meet her at the airport "to make up for the last time" Emily shot back that the client had arranged for a car service. It was a lie. Certainly, if she saved her taxi receipt, she'd be reimbursed – but she didn't tell it to Robert that way. "Already I'm embellishing," she confessed to Renee. "I haven't even seen him yet."

"What happened 'last time' at the airport?"

"He didn't show up. I didn't go back on the group flight because I wanted to spend extra days with him. He'd already decided to stay. And then he let me go to the airport myself. On the metro." Alone at the gate, she huddled on a bench, her arms wrapped around her duffle, wiping her eyes with a paper cocktail napkin. A fellow passenger, a gray-haired French woman, said to her, "*C'est difficile, quitter Paris. On peut vous aider*?" Emily had looked up at her, mutely grateful. She was nineteen. What made her miserable was less leaving Paris or even leaving Robert than returning home to a life she already anticipated would be bleak and colorless, compared to his. She was sick on the plane. But all that seemed so long ago, it was practically forgotten.

"He was only twenty then," Renee said. "Who knows what he's like now? He's living a dream." Then she cocked her head in a funny Renee-like way. "After all, that's what guys do – one last fuck for old time's sake." Old time's sake – the same phrase Robert had used.

Nothing like that happened, but still Emily felt guilty. She'd left Robert's flat at midnight, slightly drunk. After she unlocked her hotel room door, she went to lie on top of the turned-down bed, fully clothed. That was where she was when the phone rang at 6 a.m. "I know it's early there," Sandy said. "But it's midnight here and I couldn't sleep. And I was excited about a surprise I got you. Just something small," he said, "to thank you for seeing to my flute." It was only then, at 6 a.m. in her hotel room, that she realized she didn't have the flute. She'd picked it up at the shop in the Marais and then, because Robert's apartment was in the same neighborhood, kept it with her when she went to Robert's flat for dinner. Now it was morning and the flute was gone.

"You've become so French," Emily said, as she and Robert ate by candlelight.

"Not really. If you're on a budget, eating at home in Paris *c'est necessaire.*" During dinner they had spoken about his much-improved cooking (coq au vin and salad with a mustardy vinaigrette), about music, about their first meeting. They met after the French placement test, in the student lounge of Penn's Romance Languages building. Although her French was pretty good, like most of the students, she'd been stumped by the section on idioms, in which you had to explain – in French as well as English – what a particular idiom meant. The students debated whether "*pour ainsi dire*" was better translated as "so to speak" or "in a manner of speaking." Robert was the only one who recognized "*l'esprit de l'escalier*" – literally, "spirit of the staircase," meaning you thought of the right thing to say after you already left. Robert was tall and bookish and an amazing pianist; Emily found his combination of erudition and passion irresistible. In Paris, they found time to be together – in hidden corners and side rooms of the college, on park benches where they did everything "but," and finally, in a cheap hotel in the 6th, the Hotel Rose.

There they made love. At 19, it was her first time. This wasn't because she didn't want to before, but simply that she was afraid of getting pregnant. Robert was adept, unwrapping the condom with one hand while caressing her with the other. Plainly he knew what he was doing. If this meant he'd loved others before her – well, she could live with that.

"Do you remember the time the old man opened the door to our room at the Hotel Rose at midnight?" Robert asked. "You sat up and yelled, 'He's stealing our passports!' Madame came running. She explained that he'd lived there during the war, and would show up drunk and try the door. Somehow, we'd left it unlocked." They were naked under a sheet when the old man entered their room; Robert stood up with the sheet wrapped around his waist and asked the man what the hell he was doing. Emily grabbed a blanket to cover herself. Then Madame came, and Emily, who'd been yelling moments before, pretended to be asleep.

They spoke, too, about Debussy's *Children's Corner Suite,* which he would be performing at the Madeleine. "Too bad you're leaving tomorrow," he said. They used to go to those concerts. Then there were things Emily thought but didn't say. Once they agreed that if they married and had a girl, they would name her Madeleine, but Robert had said, "For my first, I want a son."

"Your French was always best in the class," she said, "and now of course it's perfect."

"I should hope so. Otherwise, what have I been up to all these years? But your errors were always so charming. Do you remember when you offered to go to the drug store for me because I had a headache? You assumed I needed aspirin. But I was out of condoms so I told you to ask the pharmacist for *une boite du preservatif.* You didn't even ask me what it was but went off and asked for it in your oh-so-careful pronunciation. The pharmacist smirked and reached under the counter, held up two packs, and asked: "*une grande boite ou une petit boite*?"

"How is it you remember what he said?" Emily asked. "You weren't even there." She'd been so angry. It was Robert's way, a joke at her expense. She fled the pharmacy and came home empty-handed. As usual, his playfulness cajoled her out of her funk, his arms around her made up for what wasn't there. "Just this once," he said. Being with him, she did things her better nature told her not to do.

How could she have left the flute behind?

She knew how. She'd gone to put her glass of water in the sink, water she'd requested to clear her head after too much wine. But he got up, too, and they collided in front of the sink; he reached his arms around her. She left quickly after that; it was no wonder she left the flute behind. Outside she found a taxi. On the way home, she boozily assessed the evening and found it, on the whole, satisfactory.

Now Robert produced two croissants from a white paper bag, chocolate oozing out of them. "I remember you loved these, Em."

He poured coffee for them both.

"I'm not hungry," she said. "I'm too worried."

"How valuable was this flute, anyway?"

"Very," she said. "It's not even mine. It's Sandy's."

"Ah," he said. "From what you've said, he can afford a replacement."

"You don't understand. This is a flute he's had for over a decade – made especially for him. It's a closed-hole flute. Pure silver, not alloy." Emily parroted the spiel she'd heard Sandy tell their friends. He ran a successful business dealing in metals and building materials, but for relaxation he played the flute. It was his passion.

"Really?" Robert paused. "Well, let's retrace your steps."

"There's nothing to retrace," she said. "After I picked up the flute, I wandered around, consulting my Paris Practique, until I found your address. My shoulder bag was over my shoulder and I had the flute case in my hand the whole time."

"You brought wine, remember. You must have stopped somewhere."

"All I remember about that store was that it was old and dusty. But I'm sure I didn't leave the flute case in the wine store. I wouldn't have." The flute was entrusted to her. It was Sandy's most prized possession.

"I have the name of the wine store, if that helps. It was on the bottle."

"Sandy will kill me. He loves – loves – that flute."

Robert came behind her, put his hands on her shoulders, and massaged gently. "*Ne paniquez pas.* He'll get over it. "

"Stop." She ducked her head, blinking back tears.

"You'll explain that you met an old flame, had dinner, and got carried away. Somehow the flute got lost in the shuffle."

He grabbed her hand. Then, as she pulled away, he placed it on the flute case.

She should have told him what she thought of him, but she didn't. When she opened the case, the flute was there, undisturbed and pristine.

"It is beautiful," Robert said. "I'm sorry, Em. I didn't realize you left it here until 3 a.m. I was waiting until 8 and then I was going to call your hotel. But when you got here you were so annoyed and brusque. Like it was my fault."

She couldn't look at him. She got up to leave.

"Can I say something? You seem to think this guy would ditch you for a flute. Is that really what you want?"

"I never said that," she said quietly.

Once she was outside, she was able to breathe.

It was only at the airport, near the gate, that the flood of sensations came back: the memory of the last time she parted from Robert. What triggered it was a young woman sitting in the departure lounge, an American girl surely, sitting by herself and crying.

Emily asked, "Are you okay?" but so softly, the girl gave no sign she heard. Then Emily saw that the girl wasn't really alone. A tall curly-haired young man paced nearby, glancing occasionally at the weeping girl. Emily didn't go over to tell him to comfort her. She didn't touch the girl on the arm. She didn't ask, so that's it, then? Or, why haven't you told him? Or, are you flying back to end it? There was no reason. There was nothing really, to make her think that this couple was like she and Robert had been. Fifteen years before, she had boarded the flight alone, she had been sick alone, alone she had discovered days later, after the bleeding finally stopped, that – had things gone differently – Robert might have had his son after all. *In a manner of speaking.*

She didn't write Robert when it happened to tell him about her pregnancy and miscarriage, and hadn't told him on this visit either. Perhaps that was why when she left Robert that morning she turned to him at the door to his flat, unable, even after his double cruelty, to say a final good-bye. She could have stopped at *au revoir*. Instead, she added an English sentence that delayed, at least for the present, the death of a secret kept. *If I'm ever back in Paris, I'll let you know.*

Reasons Why You Should or Shouldn't Sleep with Your Son's Piano Teacher

1) You will feel really terrible when he continues to expect you to pay for lessons. (CON)

2. No one makes love like a musician. You remember this from college, from a graduate student, a violinist named Seymour Katz, who looked like Groucho Marx but made love like Omar Sharif. The vibrations that Seymour Katz's long, sensitive fingers plucked from your body the body has not forgotten. (PRO)

3. He might be gay. Omar Sharif, it turned out, was gay. (CON)

4. You're still married, and even if your husband Charlie has been doing it with his paralegal for years, two wrongs don't make a right. (CON)

5. Maybe he doesn't like you, or at least not enough to have sex with you. (CON)

6. He must like you or he wouldn't have offered to stay late last Tuesday and help you with the *Mozart A Minor Rondo*. This is your favorite piece ever because it expresses a longing you didn't even know you had until you heard it. He said, "Remember, this can be as slow as you like. It's a meditation. So let it build very slowly, slowly, and then when you get here"– and he played the next passage like a wisp of smoke –"it turns into nothing." (PRO)

7. If it doesn't work out, you'll have to find Ryan a new piano teacher. (CON)

8. What kind of man becomes a piano teacher? (CON)

9. Admit that what has happened to you, to your marriage, in the last six years, has gone on too long. Charlie confessed years ago that seeing you in childbirth spoiled the marriage. "No Lamaze class on earth could have prepared me for that," Charlie said. It put him permanently off his appetite. You fell into a deep, hibernating sleep. Until recently. With Ryan reaching the Age of Reason, there is piano music in your home, and this lanky, flop-haired, soft-voiced, dreamy-eyed Southerner sitting next to you on the piano bench. (PRO or CON? – Not sure. PRO because it cancels out number 4; CON because you should devote your energy to ending the marriage, not to embarking on a *Fantaisie Impromptu* with an impecunious man ten years your junior.)

10. Where in the world is your diaphragm? Would he use a condom? Suppose he gazes intently at each of his student's mothers, helps each with her technique, secretly laughs at her clumsiness? Could you catch a disease from Mrs. Elvira Tate, whose name he gave as a reference? And where would you do it? Not in your house, certainly. Didn't he say he lived in Brooklyn? Is the neighborhood safe? Will he play for you afterwards? How out of practice are you? (CON-PRO-CON-CON-CON-CON-PRO PRO). (Yes, he will most certainly play for you afterwards. And there is only one way to find out how out of practice you are.)

You are still deciding what to do, as well as practicing more in anticipation of the piano teacher's next visit, when Ryan comes to you and confesses that, while he likes Mr. Luria and doesn't want to hurt his feelings, what he really wants to play is the guitar and would you mind if he quit piano and started guitar in the fall? Charlie says it's your fault. All that playing you were doing made the poor kid feel inadequate. Although Charlie says you give in to Ryan too much, you don't see any reason not to let the boy take up the instrument he likes.

So, when David Luria comes next Tuesday, you will explain that things have changed now, that – assuming this is okay with him – you will be the student instead of Ryan, that you place yourself in his most capable hands. And if, as you expect, he says, "Well, there will be Czerny exercises for next week but in the meantime let's go straight to the *A Minor Rondo,*" you will sit beside him and watch his fingers manipulate the passages you can't do yourself yet. You will relax your bare arm against the soft rough scratch of his sweater. You will study the way his fingers caress the arpeggios and learn what "very slowly, slowly" means.

Slowly, you will learn.

Tale of a Fish

I swallowed him whole. Yes, it was me, not Moby Dick, or one of his relatives, not a whale at all. It was me, Bibi, a Big Eye tuna fish.

There I was, minding my own business, cruising, checking out the damsel fish, when I heard God call my name. And He commanded me to swallow Jonah.

So began the longest three days and nights of my life, spent floating motionless, waiting for God to release me. God didn't tell me how long it would be for, only that I had to keep the man alive.

The glimpse I caught of Jonah before I swallowed him revealed a troubled spirit. He seemed a good man at heart, but, according to God, was trying too hard to keep a low profile. He refused to do God's bidding.

I questioned whether such a stubborn, stiff-necked man would be tender or sweet to eat in any event. But the longer Jonah was inside me, the hungrier and thirstier I became, and the harder it became to avoid consuming him. I did not want to make the same mistake Jonah had made and find myself in the belly of some sailor.

It wasn't easy. Each of my jaws contains a single row of sharp pointed teeth. And my pharynx is lined with pharyngeal teeth for tearing and chewing. Were I to duck my head, or scratch an itch, or yawn, with a single stroke I might injure or decapitate my tenant.

Yes, tenant. That's how I came to view him once I realized I couldn't make a meal of him. Kind of like a squatter. He smelled of his days at sea without fresh water for bathing and he tasted of running away and loneliness and fear. Still, I craved him.

During those three endless days and nights that Jonah was in residence, I thought a lot about my mother. I longed for her counsel. It was my mother who nicknamed me Bibi, short for my given name, Big Big. I reckoned I was her favorite. At least she always seemed to have particular concern for me. From the time I was hatched she would gaze at me with a worried look and say, "Bibi, keep a low profile."

Honestly, I tried. But when a deep, sonorous voice broke through the crashing music of the waves and called, "Bibi!" I responded, "Here I am." It was not my mother's voice.

It was God. The Bible has since reported: "Now the Lord prepared a great fish to swallow up Jonah." Great fish, mind you, not whale. I will never understand how a whale managed to get credit for my act.

I also question the use of the word "prepared," not only because it smacks of flour and seasoning, but because nothing could have prepared me for what was to follow. And God didn't even try. To be sure, He had his hands full with Jonah, whom He commanded to be a prophet and who ran off to sea instead. For me, swimming away wasn't an option. This was God, who meant business.

By the third day, the temptation of Jonah was becoming too great for me to resist. Had I tear ducts, I would have wept. Many so-called vegetarians say they make an exception for fish because fish don't have feelings. We have feelings, just no way of expressing them.

When finally, "God spake unto the fish and it vomited out Jonah upon the dry land," I again wanted to weep, this time with joy. Instead, I took off at thirty miles an hour straight to my mother.

After I broke my fast, I told my mother what had happened. She was proud of me. She told me that once when she was young, her scales shining like silver, her yellow-brown finlets edged with satiny black, a boy named Jonah had caught her and then carefully removed the hook and thrown her back. It was after that close call that she hatched me and over three hundred brothers and sisters.

"You're saying this was the same Jonah?" I asked, incredulous. "And that is why I wasn't allowed to eat him?"

"Perhaps. Perhaps not." Then she said, "Bibi, swim up to the surface for a moment and tell me what you see."

With a lunge, I obeyed, and made it to the surface and back in only two minutes. I reported to my mother that I saw a wave, in fact many waves, white-tipped and glistening.

"Where were they going?" she asked.

"Going? I couldn't tell. I saw only that they were moving and going somewhere."

"It's the same with the things we do," she said. "That boy – I'm sure his name was Jonah – couldn't know what would happen if he threw me back, and couldn't know that you would someday save the life of a man called Jonah. And I don't suppose you can know the result of saving this man, or where it will lead. You can be sure only that it will lead somewhere, and that it was the right thing to do."

As I settled down to digest my meal, I thought about my mother's words. They made it seem unimportant that some whale got the credit for being God's instrument. What had happened to me, after all, was but one roll of a wave in a constantly moving sea. Perhaps even God didn't know where the waves would lead.

After that I slept, my belly full.

Cara Cara

In a Florida hospital, I peel oranges to mask the smell of death. I sing Dad's favorite: "Gonna sit right down and write myself a letter." As a girl, I'd pictured him, young, besotted, writing endearments in florid penmanship, pretending his sweetheart (Mom?) had written the words.

Retired to Florida a decade ago, he would send Cara Cara oranges every December to Boys Town, the Doe Fund, me, lonely souls back north.

Now I sit beside his lifeless form, white-sheeted. Neither of us has anywhere to go. I sort through his mail, which he'd asked me to bring the night before. Ralph's Orange Groves has written: *Did you forget your orders this year, Morris?*

Should I tell them?

"It was time," the doctor says, stopping by to express his regrets. But the doctor didn't really know him. None of them did: not the kindest nurses, the cheerful receptionist, the jaunty mortician wandering the halls saying, "Hopefully you'll never need me, but just in case." None had heard him sing.

None had tasted those oranges, dripping with juice, cut in sections like an accordion, a suggestion in the package insert. The way Dad liked them best.

Except, of course, Ralph.

"Dear Ralph," I begin.

Morris and Cleo

We don't talk about Dad's death, my mother and I. She barely speaks at all. Instead, I go on about the weather, politics, far-flung floods and calamities. These we can bear more than the vision of my father's tear-blind eyes. Hospice-at-home, a great idea, but – too late, we realized – not for us.

I drive to the shelter in Clifton where I've heard via Petfinder about a cat needing a home. Morris (same name as Dad) is a gleaming stately beauty (orange, white-pawed), a solitary alpha male. King of the hill, they call him. His nose is raw from rubbing against the bars.

My mother leans on her walker and nods.

Thank you for giving Morris a second chance, we're told, and then told again. He is placed in a cat carrier lined with newspaper. He meows furiously.

Completing the paperwork, I see another rescue cat in a nearby cell: skinny, silver-grey, mewling. Mother follows my gaze.

"Who's that?" I ask.

Cleo.

"Anyone adopting her?"

The attendant, all smiles up to now, answers with a cagey look. Silence. She will no more speak about Cleo than my mother and I will speak about my father's death.

Cleo's eyes, liquid grief, follow us as we leave.

On the drive home, Morris's meows stop abruptly. He's asleep, but I am doubly awake. My mother's silence engulfs us.

Finally, as we pull into the driveway, she speaks. "He needs a new name," she says. "One we've never even heard of."

Heirloom

Grandson and dog arrive by Uber. The mutt, jaw clenching a ball, is as big as T.J., who's seven. "What kind of mother leaves?" my son Ollie asked when he called to say T.J. and his dog were coming for an extended visit. Ollie blames his wife, instead of his own 40-year-old folly – an injury from playing middle-aged baseball – or his go-to drug, his strike out, his oxycodone.

I don't care who's to blame. I'm too old to mother again. In my patchy backyard, T.J. throws and the mutt, plumey tail waving, bounds after. When the ball pounds my snooty neighbor's rosebushes, I run and retrieve it, relieved she isn't around. The baseball is autographed by Tino Martinez. When Ollie was in fifth grade, I stood in line outside Lord & Taylor in blistering heat to get it. "Please, mom, please," he begged. I wouldn't let him miss school but I took a sick day. In those days I'd do anything for him.

Does Ollie remember his joy? Does he know the ball is gone? Has he seen the doggie tooth marks scarring the stitching? If he did, would he care?

T.J. and the dog huddle and watch nervously, as if waiting for me to yell. My neighbor shows up on her back porch, watching, too.

So I throw the first pitch.

Yard Sale

Jackie's present to Brooke from two weeks before, *Richard Scarry's Mother Goose*, was going for two dollars. The baby shoes she bought Brooke were on offer for a pittance as well.

"Yard sale! Moving today! Last chance!" clamored the sign.

The screen door hung off its hinge. "Deirdre!" Jackie called softly to her daughter. The only sound was the baby crying. Deirdre's baby, and Tonio's. *Not yours*, Deirdre said last time. Jackie's ideas about child-rearing were antiquated, Deirdre complained, her gifts well-meaning but *off.* The pink baby shoes were kidskin, but they were raising Brooke vegan. Mother Goose was *sexist.*

When she heard they were moving to Tempe, Arizona, to be near Tonio's people, Jackie said, "I'll never get to see Brooke."

Deirdre said she could come visit. She didn't mention how hard it was for Jackie to travel: how she'd forget her tickets, or her house keys, or even where she was going. Jackie had gone to the library and looked up the city they were moving to, tried to figure out exactly how far it was from Clifton, New Jersey, but couldn't even find it on the map. An hour later, she realized she was looking for Temple, Arizona – a place that didn't even exist – when the place they were moving was *Tempe.* She was too embarrassed to tell Deirdre about her mistake, or even what she had learned from her research, which was that Tempe, Arizona was named after the Vale of Tempe in Greece, where in ancient times there was a temple to Apollo. She knew Deirdre wouldn't be interested, or at least not interested in hearing this from her.

But Jackie wasn't there for that. She came to say good-bye to them, and to the baby.

Minutes passed. Then Tonio appeared. He was small and wiry and no match for her Deirdre, who was 5'9" with large, jutting hip bones. "Brooke dozed off before I could feed her," he said wearily. "At least she stopped crying."

"Isn't Deirdre home?" Jackie asked.

"At the gym." Then he left, too, to gas-up the U-Haul.

Brooke lay on her back in her crib, awake, violet eyes blinking, forehead wrinkled in puzzlement. Jackie wanted to say "I'll make it up to you," but knew it was a lie. Your parents are your destiny, not your brain-addled Grandma.

Instead, Jackie chanted the one rhyme she could remember by heart: *"Pussycat, pussycat where have you been? I've been to London to visit the Queen. Pussycat, pussycat, what did you there? I frightened a little mouse under her chair."*

The baby watched her. She kicked her bare feet and moved her hands like birds, as if she recognized Jackie was her grandmother, as if she knew this was special, like a visitation from an angel.

"Little mouse," Jackie crooned, lifting her in her arms.

In the taxi Jackie called to speed her and Brooke to the station, she untied the baby shoes' ribbon laces, stroked the soft pink kidskin, and fitted them on.

In Memory of Maisie

At Maisie Miller's funeral, her two sons go up, one by one, falling all over themselves, like Goneril and Regan in the first act of *Lear*, proclaiming their devotion. My mother, gnarled hands in her lap, turns to me and says in a loud voice: "Maisie stole my Aloe Vera. On the Elderhostel Cruise to Cuba last year. She took it from my toiletries bag when I went to pee, and I never saw it again."

"Mom," I say, "Shush."

Maisie's older son glares at me. He hasn't looked me in the eye since seventh grade, when he pronounced me ugliest girl. He was twelve so he should, perhaps, be forgiven. Unlike Maisie, who – when my mother complained to her – said, "well, he has a point."

Mother conveyed Maisie's response without hesitation–unable, even then, to keep things to herself.

"That one lives in Beijing," Mother says, pointing to the younger son, "so he doesn't have to see Maisie."

"He's certainly seeing her now," I stage-whisper to Mother, beginning to share her venomous mood. "All dolled up like a ghoul in that open casket."

When we were kids, the Beijing boy wasn't as verbal as his older brother but was notorious for snapping bras. I got snapped so often, I switched to front closure before they were popular.

Maisie's six-year-old granddaughter is speaking now. "I loved Granny," the little girl says, "because her cheeks were soft and she smelled like . . ."

"Aloe Vera!" shouts my mother. Maisie's older son turns around and whispers, "Can't you control the old crow?"

"She smelled like cookies," the girl finishes, with an exaggerated curtsy.

"Where do you think those soft cheeks came from?" My mother in her wheelchair, in a black sequined sweater, glitters with rage. "I wouldn't have minded if she borrowed it, but this was pure thievery."

Everyone is turning around now and telling me to shut her up. The minister, oblivious, asks if anyone else has something to say.

I think then not of *Lear*, but of *Hamlet: The croaking raven doth bellow for revenge.*

So I stand up and say, "My mother would like the floor."

Fifty Cents A Cap

It was the librarian's most prized children's book. Her grandson Omer clamored for it from age two. Together they shouted their favorite lines. The school children loved *Caps for Sale* too: the peddler with caps piled on his head, the thieving monkeys in their tree. She taught them about the author and artist, Esphyr Slobodkina, whose first name was pronounced *es-fear*, who fled Russia with her Jewish family when she was only nine. The librarian threw around words like *avant-garde* hoping some of them would stick.

In December, 32-year-old Omer visits his grandmother, now 98 and tiny as an elf under blankets on the settee. "Open your eyes, grandma!" They light up then, one eye squinty, the other round and surprised. Blue as the Atlantic they waded in hand in hand, their skin slippery with sunscreen, their feet – his tender, hers hardened and hammer-toed – seeking soft purchase among the shells and small rocks.

"What's on your head?" she asks.

"My wool cap. It's cold out, Grandma."

They examine it together. "Nice," she says. "Warm." She grabs with bony fingers and hides it under the blankets.

"Give me back my cap!" he yells, like the peddler in the book. "Tsz," she cries, as hoarse as the monkeys in their tree. "Tsz." He reaches under the blankets. Tickled with laughter, she punches his arm. He battles bone and knob, no softness there but wool. Victorious, he plumps the cap graciously on his grandma's balding head.

They giggle so hard he has to stop her from falling off the settee, from rolling away, from taking him with her to the next chapter.

Yahrzeit

The sun is blinding so I put on my shades. Alma shifts in her chair. By now, I know what the shifting means. You can't wear sunglasses during therapy. Maybe if you're a sullen teenage girl, dragged in by a desperate mother: *top girl student, refusing to attend her graduation*. But not that same daughter, forty years later, a year after her mother's death.

"Let me pull the blind." Alma leaves her yellow notepad uncovered. With my sunglasses off, I can't not look. I have a wandering eye. This got me in trouble in school. I didn't look at my neighbor's work to copy it; always, my pen was down. My classmates didn't understand. Elliot covered his paper. Gail yelled, "Cathy is copying!" That was worse than getting sent to the principal, worse than my mother's distress when the principal telephoned her. *Top girl student, copying*?

On her pad, Alma has scrawled *Kathi S.*; *aversion to tapping, Yarzite*. After a year, she still misspells my name. If I mention it, she'll know I looked. Besides, what's the big deal? She misspelled *Yahrzeit*, too. That's different, of course. A Yiddish word. Alma isn't Jewish. And Jewish or not Jewish, who knows how to spell Yahrzeit?

I clear my throat, my *shtick* like chair-shifting is hers. "Maybe I should do tapping." A way to distract myself from the clandestine viewing of her notes, from her mistakes, from my own.

I hate tapping. Hate its pseudoscientific nomenclature: *Emotional Freedom Technique*. Hate the jargon about ephemeral energy patterns you're supposed to create, or maybe destroy.

Hate the mantra you recite as you tap different pathways in your body. The mantra is personal. It always makes me feel worse. *A fraud.* "Even though my mother suffered a painful death, I deeply and completely accept myself." Talk about bullshit. If that were true, would I be in Alma's office every Friday? For months I've obsessed over the things I should have attended to but didn't: *Her allergy to morphine. Her doctor's mistakes. Her fear.*

Alma knows I abhor tapping. She doesn't want to go there. "It's a year since your mother died, isn't it?"

Her death. "See you tomorrow," I said the night before. By then mom was nearly gone, her breathing slowed, the monitors off. Silence. I could have stayed; she would have stayed if our roles were reversed. Instead, I told her I'd be back at eight. The next morning, she died at 8:01. Creeping like a snail, like the reluctant schoolboy in Jaques' ages of man, I arrived at 8:13.

Sometimes Alma uses a different technique, a nameless one. She shares her own guilt about her husband's death two years before. The first time, I wondered what happened to the silent, poker-faced shrink, like the man my mother took me to see when I was sixteen. But Alma's strategy is strangely comforting. Her *what if's* rival mine. *What if I had refused his last intubation? What if I hadn't taken the subway that morning? What if I had yelled at Dr. Lee instead of being so polite?* Our second-guessing tropes are like echoes in a cave.

Now she asks: "What's that word you used last week? The Yiddish one?" I know the word she means. I saw it, misspelled, in her notes.

"Yahrzeit. Time of year. The anniversary of the death." Am I telling her anything she doesn't know? I reach in my bag and retrieve the squat white candle in a glass cup."I'll light it tonight. It burns 24 hours. Tomorrow in synagogue, they'll call me up to chant the memorial prayer, say her name. Every year on her Yahrzeit. They knew her there."

Alma nods, jots something down. I lean forward but can't read it.

When she looks up her eyes are glassy. "We have nothing like that. First year, nothing. Second year, nothing. Smoke and ashes. Then nothing."

She begins crying full on, shielding her eyes, her head bowed.

I stand up, then sit down. Going to her would be crazy. "I'm tapping," I say loudly. I omit the mantra, start right in. I use karate chops: first my forehead, then my cheek, then my chin. I don't know if she hears me; her head is still down. When I get to my chest, I go for it. It's more than mere tapping, more like the *mea culpas* we do on Yom Kippur. I feel better, pounding my heart. The only sound in the room.

"Quit tapping," she says, so I stop.

We stare at each other in the silence. We rest.

Mayim

The Lubavitch Hasidim are sending two teen volunteers to spend time with our daughter. I resist at first, but Mattie's Special Ed teacher explains that it's a mitzvah for the girls, who are 16, a special program started by a rabbi's wife. She says I should let them come; it might be good for Mattie. She hasn't seen Mattie smile in the eight months since her mom died.

If Kayla were alive, she would have fumed: "We're not religious. What will they do with Mattie? Pray?" But when I say this to the Special Ed teacher, she says you don't have to be religious to qualify for a visit. You don't even have to be Jewish.

Without Kayla's moxie, I give in.

I miss her too.

A half-hour before they're due, Mattie's running circles in our parched backyard. "My friends are coming, my friends are coming!" She's ten, barefoot, friendless. The play dates I arrange don't return, too sad, too weird, too slow. They want to talk about *Harry Potter*. She's stuck on *Katy No-Pocket.*

It's been a dry Spring and I keep forgetting to water the yard. The bottoms of Mattie's feet are already caked with dirt. The doorbell rings. No time to do anything about that.

"Dad, they're here!" Mattie races to greet them, ballerina skirt and pink top glittering. Talia and Deb, longhaired, long-skirted, grin at her. "Hi, Mattie! Nice meeting you. What pretty hair! What a pretty skirt!"

I am determined not to eavesdrop, to let them be. I offer them lemonade but they have brought their own bottles of Poland Spring, and one for Mattie, too. Meanwhile I finish the laundry.

Sometime after I've hung the delicates to dry, the girls turn on an ancient CD player they've brought. They remove their shoes like Mattie and join hands with her in a circle dance. The word "mayim" repeats endlessly: *mayim, mayim, mayim, mayim, hey mayim bisason*! I have heard this song, seen this dance, at a wedding or Bar Mitzvah, but don't know what it means. Although I don't ask, a breathless Talia translates for my benefit. "Water of joy," she says. "Pioneers found water in the desert after seven years. Somebody wrote a song." Eventually the music ends. All three girls collapse laughing in a heap.

Mattie's childish underpants – embroidered with the days of the week – hang on the clothesline alongside another ballerina skirt and matching tights. My wife and I often talked about whether Mattie would always stay a child. I no longer consider the question. Talia and Deb gather their shoes and the CD player. Will they come back?

Mattie hums, practicing a step.

Then the girls chorus: "See you next week!"

Our daughter's clothes rustle in the dry wind. The ballerina skirt balloons like a sail. If I were religious, I might say a prayer of thanks or of hope. But I don't even know a prayer.

Instead, I whisper *mayim*.

Dream Job

Alice's new office faced south, overlooking the public library and Fifth Avenue. From the window she saw her favorite lion, *Fortitude*, guarding the library's north steps. The office wasn't large but that first day following her promotion, it was perfect. The furniture was new. Gone was the scratched wood desk with its modesty panel. The dingy walls, scarred by thumbtacks, were gone, too. Instead, there was a sleek steel desk with elegant red enameled drawers; pale grey walls (a color called seashell); an aura of competence and calm.

Gustave Caillebotte's *Paris Street: Rainy Day*, a gift from her boss, graced one wall.

You bring kindness and patience to every interview, Philip Massie said when he promoted her, in her seventh year with the company. Her door was always open, *another hallmark*, Massie said. *You share information. You don't hoard it.* The agency Massie founded in 1985, *Career Builders,* placed temps to fill in for employees on leave. Career Builders vetted and interviewed applicants so companies didn't have to. For Alice's clients, those temporary positions often became permanent.

"Nice digs, huh?" Massie's white shirt was patched with sweat, his brown curls sodden. The a/c was on, but low, an energy-saving measure, emblem of the times. Massie looked at his watch. "Your first intake is in fifteen minutes. Liana Broder."

"I'm ready," Alice said brightly.

"Don't forget, party at three." They were celebrating both the move to 500 Fifth *and* her promotion. Alice had a full day of meetings until then.

"So, who you rooting for, Venus or Serena?"

"I'm an older sister. Venus, for sure."

"117 years ago – Wimbledon women's final, 1884 – Maud Williams beat her kid sister Lilian. Maybe you're right."

Fifteen minutes later, Liana Broder stood before the painting. "Where *is* that? Wait! It's Paris, right?"

"Paris in the rain. Have a seat, Liana. I'm Alice."

"This is weird, but it reminds me of a sepia photograph. I love photography, love art, all sorts. Sorry, I'm jabbering. I should be quiet so you can read my stuff."

"Not a problem," Alice had already read Liana's application but reviewed it again, to let Liana get settled. To see how she handled silence. Liana – slender and petite, with curly black hair, intense blue eyes, and a strong handshake -- wore a rust-colored tweed suit, a white top, a tear-shaped brooch on her lapel: topaz, her birthstone. She was among Alice's best applicants in her age group (early 20s): high school valedictorian, 3.6 GPA from Stonybrook, English major. Glowing references. Only a few gaps on the application. In response to *Where do see yourself in five years?* she had typed *unsure. Dream job*, she left blank.

The interview lasted an hour. Alice pressed Liana on her goals. Travel – to Paris, to London, to India – was one of Liana's dreams. But her dream job eluded her. "Something creative. Perhaps everyone says that. Acting or film-making or even writing."

Liana and applicants like her were the reason Alice's work mattered. Liana could tell Alice the truth. She didn't have to feign enthusiasm for a company or business she knew nothing about. Maybe she'd learn to love it – much as Alice found her own niche in career placement.

Not much glamour there. But satisfaction of a kind, so long as you didn't want too much.

"My sister's an actress," Alice said to Liana. Sharing personal details encouraged applicants to open up. Knowledge – about the applicant, the jobs, hiring trends – was key. "Unless you hit it big, it's not easy. I'm sure you know that. My sister keeps trying but it's been hard." Alice's parents had supported her sister financially for years, dazzled by the notion of Beth's acting career. "In the meantime, you're making the right decision to explore other options. *And* make some dough."

Liana laughed and seemed to relax. Alice's screen displayed two jobs: a low-paying three-week gig in publicity at a midtown publishing house, and one downtown, in the financial district, at Cantor Fitzgerald.

"Which do *you* recommend?" Liana asked.

Although the publishing house was more in Liana's field of interest, Alice found herself pushing Cantor Fitzgerald. "The offices are beautiful, the people more down-to-earth than you might expect from financial services. The location is amazing. 105th floor of the World Trade Center. That in itself is special. They're looking for someone super organized. A decent writer."

"I love making order out of chaos *and* I love to write."

Alice dialed Cantor HR. She rattled off Liana's strengths. It was arranged. Liana would begin a month-long stint there the next week. Her first day would be Monday, September 10th.

"Let me know how it goes."

"You mean Monday?"

"Not necessarily Monday – only if there's a problem. But later in the week, give me a call. I'd love to hear from you."

Before she left, Liana stood in front of the Caillebotte. "It's funny how all the umbrellas are identical. And the cobblestones look like they're floating."

"And slippery," Alice said. "Conveyed with a mere brush stroke."

In the hour they were together, she'd grown fond of Liana Broder.

Tuesday came. Alice was in her office by 8:30. Fifteen minutes later, the phone rang. When she picked it up no one was there. "Hello?" she asked. "Hello?"

Whoever it was, was cut off. Then Massie appeared at the threshold of her office, his face ashen, eyes glassy. "Come, Alice. We're in the conference room. The TV is on there."

When she arrived, 15-odd staffers were gathered. Some were crying.

It was Liana's second day at Cantor Fitzgerald. She would have arrived early to get her boss's files in shape. Organizing them so he'd be ready for his meetings.

At that moment, Alice still hoped for the best. Surely the girl would be fine. Surely, she would be.

Fine.

# # #

Fifteen years later, Philip Massie stood in the doorway of Alice's stripped-down office. "One more intake?" he asked. "Please?" His smile was as beguiling as ever; his gray curls spiraled over his shirt collar. On Alice's desk sat a blue vase of yellow roses. "Good-bye and good luck!" read the card. Alice's belongings were in boxes. Her desk, except for the computer terminal, was bare.

Next door, in the conference room, balloons floated, tied to a red plastic bucket and shovel. Alice was moving to Southern California, where her parents, sister, and 16 year-old nephew lived. There was prosecco on ice, strawberries, brie, a sheet cake. But the party wouldn't start for 90 minutes. "Okay, hand it over."

Massie leaned over her desk, sniffed the roses. Alice inhaled, instead of roses, the faint scent of Old Spice the man always wore. Like Alice, Massie was a dinosaur. "Her name is Amy Lawrence. I think you'll like her. She's what? 23 or 24. Only a few years younger than you when you started here. She's interested in executive assistant spots, something financial." Alice's mind was so bound up with leaving it was difficult to imagine giving the spiel one more time.

When Amy Lawrence walked into Alice's office, Alice was sorry she said yes. It was no fault of Ms. Lawrence. Her voice was soft but confident. She had smooth, honey-colored skin, light hazel eyes, and slightly coarse black hair that curled neatly to her shoulders. Her tweed suit brought out her eyes. But Alice found it hard to focus. She knew she wasn't imagining the resemblance between Amy Lawrence and the other young woman, Liana Broder–only the eye color was different.

"Sorry about my office. Mr. Massie might have told you. After 22 years, I'm heading out west."

"He said you're the best, that I was lucky to meet with you."

"You get credit for knowing what you want. Executive assistant in the financial sector. That makes it easier." Amy's resume included BMCC associate degree, Spanish, Maria in Clara Barton High School's *West Side Story*. The Spanish might be helpful, and her skills were good. "You've got Microsoft Office, PowerPoint, Excel. Just what you need."

When Alice saw the three openings on her screen, she couldn't speak at first. Finally, she said: "Why don't you come take a look."

Amy stood behind her. "Is any of them a hedge fund? I've heard they're the place to go if you want to make money." She gave a slight, self-deprecating laugh.

"Albrecht is. The other two are brokerage houses, Morgan Stanley and Cantor Fitzgerald. I'm sure you've heard of them. The positions are long-term temporary and roughly equivalent – administrative assistant to a mid level manager. Covering for someone on maternity leave. Actually," she paused, "at Albrecht it's to replace somebody on *paternity* leave."

"That's cool. Replacing a guy."

With Liana, Alice spent more time getting to know her. Then, as now, it was a Friday and there was a party that afternoon. Unlike Amy, Liana hadn't listed anything under *dream job* on her application. Unlike Amy, she had no answer for *where you want to be in five years.*

"If it's Albrecht you want," Alice told Amy Lawrence, "I should call right away. They close early on Fridays."

Amy said, "Go ahead." After a brief phone conversation, it was set. Before Amy left, Alice handed her a business card. Her own name was blacked out; the contact information for her two most experienced colleagues was handwritten below. "Call either one if you have questions."

Whatever you do, she thought, don't call me.

Before the party, Alice went to freshen up. While she was in the stall, two women entered the ladies' room. "Are you staying for Alice's party?" she heard Marie (who placed medical assistants) ask Patricia, whom Alice had trained.

"I wanted to but I have a big date. Getting my hair blown out, makeup done, the works. I'll miss her, though."

"Well," said Marie, "with Alice gone there'll be more commissions for the rest of us."

"Tell me about it! But if it wasn't for those commissions, she'd still be here, plugging away."

"Don't you think she'll get a job out there? If I know Alice, she will. I can't imagine her not working."

"Then why is she leaving?"

"I always thought she was half in love with Massie. Not that she'd ever have an affair. But admiring him, putting him on a pedestal. But then Mrs. Massie goes and dies and he's single. The fantasy evaporates. At least that's one theory."

Alice stayed in the stall until they left. Given her longevity at the company, gossip was inevitable, she reasoned. They didn't know the truth. They didn't know she had placed Liana Broder. They didn't know Philip Massie helped her through it. Alice looked at the mirror over the trio of sinks as she washed her hands. It was cracked and mottled in the lower right-hand corner. *Distressed.* She'd read a review in the Times the night before of a restaurant where the walls were flanked by distressed mirrors. This was now a much-emulated style – folks sought it in their furniture, like teenagers (her 16 year-old nephew, for example), who purchased ripped and faded jeans. Occasionally a job candidate came to interview with Alice dressed that way, or with three earrings in each ear, or heavily tattooed. Alice would gently explain that, when it came to the jobs in her book, the applicant had to present something different – even if it meant being untrue to one's true self. Years before, she would speak about the value of working in and experiencing an environment that, at first glance, was outside your comfort zone. She would explain the difference between style and substance; how you could love Shakespeare or Bach or Brecht but still find a home in a corporate environment, even find like-minded colleagues.

Now, she would simply say, "You need to work on your image before we send you out on a job."

The crack in the mirror had been there for years. It was strange to think she wouldn't be seeing it every day, as strange as taking the subway to work that morning for the last time. Every weekday since she started at the firm, she'd taken the 1 train to 42nd Street and then the shuttle. Often, she arrived at Grand Central without being able to remember boarding the two trains that got her there. If someone asked her directions as she exited the train, she couldn't even say where she was for the moment. Her body had memorized the route. It was in her blood. Now she was cutting the bloodline.

Then Alice did something she rarely did during all her years at the firm. She closed her office door. She sat on the floor and opened one of the boxes, leafed through several red-welds. But she didn't find the photograph, not right away. First, she found the letter Philip Massie wrote to her, a few weeks after September 11, when she tried to resign. By then Liana's presence in the North Tower, and her death there, had been confirmed. Alice had stopped going to work. She stopped going anywhere. His letter asked her to stay on. Eventually, she did. At the time she thought it wasn't because of his letter or even out of loyalty. Rather, it was the prospect of having to explain to a prospective employer why she left. She couldn't lie.

And so she returned to the new office, to the view from her window of *Fortitude*, to the Caillebotte, to the color known as *seashell.*

For a while she went to a counselor, paid for by Philip Massie. But the counselor couldn't help with the dreams. Funny enough, these were dreams, not nightmares. In the dreams, she interviewed Liana and sent her to a different job. Sometimes the job was the publishing house stint that had been available that Friday. Sometimes it was in a real estate office, which weren't even jobs Alice handled. Once she got a part for

Liana in a play. Liana came by to thank her. Alice cupped her hand over her phone receiver, said it was Liana's own qualities that got her the role, not anything Alice did.

Once she dreamed they were in Paris together. It was raining. Liana slipped on wet cobblestones. Alice caught her.

The dreams lasted for months.

The clipping from the *Times*, when Alice found it, was neatly folded. It had a paragraph about Liana as well as a photo. It said September 11th was her second day, that she was a temp employee. Liana's 17-year-old brother was quoted. He spoke about Liana's optimism. How she always looked forward to September. Even when it rained, she loved the excitement in the air. Something new about to happen.

Fifteen years after the Friday she interviewed Liana Broder, on her last day at work, Alice folded the *Times* clipping in an envelope. When she took her suit jacket to the dry cleaner that weekend, she found it.

Always after that she would put it somewhere safe and find it unexpectedly.

There I Will Take Your Hand

A matinee at the Met, followed by dinner. A grandfather's dream. Sixth row balcony, unobstructed view. *Don Giovanni.* Five minutes to curtain, the seat next to me still empty. Then, a soft commotion at the aisle; even softer apologies to the people she disturbs to get there. "I'm sorry I'm late," Lorna says. "Believe it or not, I'm coming from the office." After she settles in, she reports what the usher said: the last-minute substitute for Zerlina is better than the original.

The chandeliers begin their slow ascent.

"A gift from your cursed *Wienna.* Isn't that what you always say about the chandeliers, Grandpa?"

"Indeed." During intermission, we find a good spot to people-watch, a ledge for me to lean on. I unwrap four Lorna Doone cookies. Same as when she was ten, we eat them with milk pilfered from the coffee station. "Is it wrong Grandpa," she asked at ten (such a serious child!), "to take the milk when we haven't bought coffee?" I told her that in *Wienna*, they served coffee during the interval to everyone; in summer, ice cream.

"Dinner tonight will be unusual," Lorna warns. "All seven species of trees, from figs to olives. For the holiday." What holiday? But I don't ask. Then it's the second act and the final scene: sinful Don Giovanni consumed in flames.

"That's one weird opera." Lorna's studio apartment is nearby, but even the six-block walk exhausts me. "The music is beautiful, but the story? I get why you didn't take me as a kid."

What operas did I take her to as a child? *The Magic Flute*, for sure. *Hansel and Gretel*? A kiddie version of *Barber of Seville*? It's been 20 years.

"Did you see *Don Giovanni* when you lived in Vienna, Grandpa? With your parents?"

"I'm not sure," I say. "It's one of my favorites."

"I know you saw *Fidelio* and *Fledermaus*. You always mentioned them." She takes my coat, fusses in the kitchenette, arranges two place settings on the bridge table. Meanwhile, Simone – my cat for a decade, before Assisted Living made me give her up – is going crazy, circling my legs, meowing, then purring nonstop.

"Forget me, forget Mozart, you're all about Simone, Grandpa."

My daughter Helene once said, in front of Lorna, that I shouldn't make things up. "You were six when you left Vienna on Kindertransport. You didn't go to operas. Why do you tell Lorna such things?" I didn't deny what Helene said; but didn't admit it either. Lorna said, "I believe Grandpa. You weren't there, mom, you don't know."

Lorna gives me a printed menu she prepared at her office. It describes the seven species and their significance, along with the bill of fare: mushroom barley soup, olive bread, salad with grapes, fig gelato. At the top: Grandpa and Lorna's Tu B'Shvat Dinner.*That* holiday. *The birthday of the trees.* Obscure; nearly forgotten. I'm impressed Lorna knows about it.

She serves me pomegranate juice, symbolizing majesty. "What do you think?"

"Nothing a little wodka can't fix."

She grins, pours a jigger. The alcohol loosens my tongue. Or perhaps it's the CD she puts on. *La Ci Darem La Mano*. Out of context, the Don's attempted seduction of Zerlina falls away. The music is pure longing. Anticipating loss for what isn't going to happen.

"What does the song mean, again?"

"The first line means *there I will take your hand.*"

That's the line, I want to say. *The rest doesn't matter.* I am 88 years old. "I must tell you something. Before I forget. It's about my sister. She was four years older." Lorna's face is rapt, like she doesn't want to miss a word. "They took *her* to the opera. Not me. I was too little. After they got home, she would come to my room and tell me everything."

Lorna turns off the CD. "That's better." She asks if Helene knows I had a sister. I shake my head. She says: "Don't cry."

"That's what *she* said. My sister. She was supposed to go on Kindertransport, but got a cough or a sore throat, something, enough to make them reject her. My parents had nothing left. They made me go instead. Simone said: *Don't cry, Abilah, I'll come find you. You'll look up, and I'll be there, reaching for your hand. I promise.*"

"*Simone*, Grandpa? Her name was *Simone*?"

The cat is at the window, bristling at a pigeon through fogged glass. Indifferent to the sound of her name.

Yes, I tell my granddaughter.

Simone.

ACKNOWLEDGMENTS AND THANKS

I'm indebted to the following publications, in which these stories first appear, sometimes with a different title or in a slightly different form.

100 Word Story: "How My Mother Lost Her Voice and Gave Me Mine"

Amsterdam Quarterly: "Cara Cara"

And We Pass Through (UK National Flash Fiction Anthology 2019): "Complicity"

Bath Flash Fiction Anthologies 2017, 2018, 2019, 2020:"Clementine"; "Learning to Dive in Bonaire"; "Foley Square, July 2019"; "Ski In/Ski Out"

Blue Fifth Review: "Destiny"

Blue Monday Review: "Family Day" *

Brighton Prize Anthology: "Morris and Cleo *

Cahoodaloodaling:: "End Game"

Ekphrastic Review: "At the Pool Party for My Niece's Graduation from Middle School"; The Decision" *

Electric Literature: "So Gentle You Don't Feel It"

Fish Anthology 2015: "Tiffy" *

Flash Frontier: "Reading, Writing, Arithmetic"

Gemini: "Breakfast with Henry" *; "13 Tips for Photographing Your Nephew's Bar Mitzvah When You Still Can't Forgive Your Brother-in-Law" *

Green Mountains Review: "After the Wedding"

Jellyfish Review: "Hal's Sleep Showroom"

KYSO Flash: "Collateral Damage''; "Heirloom"; "Hide-and-Seek"; "No Offense" (in Spanish as "Sin offender" and published in *Instantaneas de ficcion,* Argentina)

La Presa:: "Fifty Cents a Cap" (in Spanish as "Cincuenta centavos por gorra")

Literal Latte: "Adventureland"

Litro: "A Bohemian Memoir"; "Dream Job"

Mid-American Review: "Fathers" *

Nano Fiction: "Waiting" (published as "1973")

New Guard Review: "Spirit of the Staircase"

New Orleans Review: "In Memory of Maisie"

Night Train: "Bar Mitzvah"; "Eavesdropping" *

North American Review: “Security Device”
The Offbeat: “Now You See It”
Orca Lit: “Yahrzeit”; “There I Will Take Your Hand”
Parabola: “Tale of a Fish”
The Phare: “St Malo”
Potpourri: “Reasons Why You Should or Shouldn’t Sleep with Your Son’s Piano Teacher”
Retreat West: “Do You Remember Me?”*
River Styx “First Night”* (reprinted in *Best Small Fictions 2016*)
R.K.V.R.Y: “Yard Sale”
Southeast Review: “Ecosystem”*
Streetlight Magazine “Mayim”* (selected for *Best Small Fictions 2022*): “Susceptible to Scratches”*
Vestal Review: “After Happiness”

*The asterisked stories were prize-winners or finalists in the respective publications.

Thanks to the editors of these wonderful publications who believed in my work and to the workshops and teachers that encouraged me to keep writing, especially Beth Ann Bauman’s Filling the Well and the Kenyon Review summer workshops; writing mentors Karen Bender, Wyn Cooper, and the late, great Nancy Zafris; and Pamela Painter, my first flash fiction teacher.

Thanks to Jean Arambula and Roberta George of Snake Nation Press, photographer Chrystie Sherman for the cover photograph, and Paul Arambula, for his work on the design of the book.

Thanks to my writing buddies: Kit Irwin, of longest standing; Jeanette Topar; and the members of Joan Colen’s writing group.

Special thanks to my son Jonah Peppiatt, who first conceived of my work as a collection a decade ago.

The greatest thanks, now and always, go to my husband Malcolm Spector, who read every story many times and lived and breathed this book with me.

THE AUTHOR

From a wedding night's unsettling revelations to a grandfather's secret to a reckoning on a French beach, Nancy Ludmerer's characters move from loss to repair in unexpected ways. Nancy's stories, including many prizewinners, have appeared in *Electric Literature, Gemini, Kenyon Review, Mid-American Review, North American Review, New Orleans Review, Orca Lit, Streetlight,* and in anthologies in Ireland, the Netherlands, the UK, and Argentina. Her flash fiction has been translated into Spanish, read aloud on public radio, and selected for *Best Small Fictions 2016 and 2022.* Other stories have won prizes from *Carve, Masters Review, Pulp Literature,* and *Orison Books*. Her non-fiction appears in *The American Lawyer, Vogue, Green Mountains Review,* and *Brain, Child,* and her short memoir "Kritios Boy" (*Literal Latte*) was cited in *Best American Essays 2014*. Nancy practiced law in New York City for many years while raising her son as a single mom, writing stories late at night or on weekends, and only recently turned to writing full-time. She lives in NYC with her husband Malcolm and their 13-year-old cat, Joey.

Collateral Damage

Nancy Ludmerer

Winner of the 2022

Serena McDonald Kennedy Fiction Award

Previous Winners

Dwight Yates	*Haywire Hearts and Slide Trombones*	2006
Brian Bedard	*Grieving on the Run*	2007
Kathy Flann	*Smoky Ordinary*	2008
Wendy Marcus	*Polyglot*	2009
Starkey Flythe	*Driving With Hand Controls*	2010
Richard Fellinger	*They Hover Over Us*	2011
Dwight Holing	*California Works*	2012
John Zeugner	*Under Hiroshima, Collected Stories*	2013
Jacob M. Appel	*The Magic Laundry*	2014
Misty Urban	*A Lesson in Manners*	2015
Carol Roan	*A Change in the Air*	2018

Serena McDonald Kennedy

Serena McDonald Kennedy was born in 1850 on the fourth of July. She was the fifth of seven daughters and the ninth of 12 children, of James and Serena Swain McDonald in Thomas County, Georgia. She was descended from Alexander McDonald, a Scottish Highlander, who fought with General James Oglethorpe at the Battle of Bloody Marsh, which saved Florida from the Spanish. His son was our Revolutionary hero.

Her father and mother, after marriage, settled on a farm between the McDonald and Swain plantations, later occupying the Reese plantation and finally the Swain plantation where they lived until their deaths. A town grew up around their home site named McDonald, Georgia, now known as Pavo, making James one of the first real estate developers of the area.

Serena, although far down the list of girls, had her mother's name, one, it was said, that fit her personality. Only a few years after her birth, her father would go to war as a Lieutenant-Colonel in the Confederacy, and she would lose a brother in the War Between the States. We have in our possession a long letter written in beautiful Spencerian script from her brother, Kenneth, a Captain, on April 20, 1863 (when she was 13 and he was 23), from "near Fredricksburg, Virgina." He wrote of the beauty* of Spring in Virginia, and as a postscript, he said: "You will excuse this miserable bad written thing of a letter; for God's sake don't show it." Only two weeks later, he was wounded at Chancellorsville and died three weeks later.

Serena was 30 years old before McDonald, Georgia, became Pavo, because of a conflict with the larger town named McDonough. At that time, a Mr. Peacock was Postmaster, and wanted the town to have his name, so in forwarding a group of names for selection to the U.S. Postal Service, he included Pavo (Latin for "peacock") and was the one chosen. At 35,

Serena was what was then generally called "an old maid," who came to the community of Enon in Thomas County as a school teacher. There she met and married John Thomas Kennedy, ten years her junior. Tom, as he was called, had lost a young wife and child in childbirth, and he and Serena began a life together that lasted for 40 years, until Serena died at the age of 75. Tom died 10 years later. They were the parents of four children, the second of whom was my father, Archibald Randolph Kennedy.

My grandmother was a great believer in education, and to our ultimate benefit, she saw that my father went to prep school and college, unusual in the rural area in which our family lived. His education influenced our family in many ways, and I attribute my love of literature to that heritage.

Although Serena died before I was born, my mother, Adeline Kennedy, was so devoted to her mother-in-law that she quoted her often and patterned our development after what she learned from her mother-in-law. My sister, Martha Stephenson, my brother, William Kennedy, and I are her only grandchildren living today. It is a great honor for us to have the Serena McDonald Kennedy Award named for her.

-Barbara Kennedy Passmore

The weather has turned warm and pleasant at last. The cold icy blast of winter has past and all nature looks revived. The sufferings of a cold hard winter seem to have been all forgotten and a few warm days have induced the trees to put forth their Buds and Blossoms. Everything seems to be in a high state of pleasure and glee. Everything is beautiful and harmonious. It's a bright Sabbath morning..."

–Kenneth McDonald

More Praise for *Collateral Damage*

At times hilarious, at other times heartbreaking, Nancy Ludmerer's masterful *Collateral Damage* is essential reading for fans of emotionally resonant fiction. Here you'll find forty-eight tales of redemption, loss, yearning and regret, of the sacrifices big and small we make to remain connected. Ludmerer writes with deep understanding of the nuanced frailties of human relations.

ALICE KALTMAN, author of *Dawg Towne*

Collateral Damage is a page turner, not that these trim, witty, unpredictable stories shouldn't be savored. Nancy Ludmerer's keen sense of how, in short form, to craft endings that pay off is one of the triumphs of this book. And, while flash fiction is a form that can make magic from one note stories, her work is at once brief and complex.

STUART DYBEK, author of *Paper Lantern: Love Stories*

Collateral Damage features characters full of longing: to be loved, to be desired, to be noticed, and to be remembered. In just a page or two, Nancy Ludmerer shines a spotlight on pivotal moments of understanding and epiphany. These are stories about characters failing in their responsibilities to others, secrets kept, and moments when relationships dissolve. Yet these stories are also about characters hoping for something better in their lives and brief moments of joy and connection. Ludmerer accomplishes so much in these small, crystalline stories.

KARIN LIN-GREENBERG, author of *Vanished*

What goes on when the doors are closed and the shades drawn? In Nancy Ludmerer's world it's not happiness and board games. It's mean-spirited or hapless husbands, angry wives, and troubled families – all written as only Ludmerer can write them in *Collateral Damage*. In "Hal's Sleep Showroom" a couple's efforts to find the perfect mattress reveal deeper yearnings. In "Security Device" a young widow purchases a blow-up doll to deter carjackers, but it becomes – well, read it and see. "In Memory of Maisie" turns a funeral into a fiasco. But don't take my word for it. Buy the book plus one for a friend because you won't want to lend this out.

PAUL BECKMAN, author of *Kiss Kiss*